P9-CFQ-989

"I would have helped with Brodie." The words shot out of his mouth before he could stop them.

Shayla shifted in her seat to face him. "You accused my father and brother of being criminals, remember?"

Mike couldn't deny it.

More miles passed before he spoke again. "I want to be a part of Brodie's life."

Shayla let out a harsh laugh. "I'm sure you do. However, has it occurred to you that the two people you're accusing of being criminals are Brodie's uncle and grandfather?"

A hard lump formed in the back of his throat, making it impossible to speak. She was right—he hadn't considered that fact, yet he couldn't let go of what he knew in his heart was true. Duncan and Ian were involved in his father's murder and needed to be brought to justice.

No matter the consequences? His resolve wavered. He couldn't lose his son.

"Yeah, that's what I thought," Shayla said in a weary tone.

He knew he needed to tread lightly. Alienating Shayla wouldn't help his goal of being involved in Brodie's life.

Laura Scott is a nurse by day and an author by night. She has always loved romance, and read faith-based books by Grace Livingston Hill in her teenage years. She's thrilled to have published over twelve books for Love Inspired Suspense. She has two adult children and lives in Milwaukee, Wisconsin, with her husband of thirty years. Please visit Laura at laurascottbooks.com, as she loves to hear from her readers.

Books by Laura Scott

Love Inspired Suspense

Callahan Confidential

Shielding His Christmas Witness
The Only Witness
Christmas Amnesia
Shattered Lullaby
Primary Suspect
Protecting His Secret Son

Military K-9 Unit

Battle Tested

Classified K-9 Unit

Sheriff

Visit the Author Profile page at Harlequin.com for more titles.

PROTECTING HIS SECRET SON

LAURA SCOTT

HARLEQUIN® LOVE INSPIRED® SUSPENSE

If you purchased this book without a cover you should be aware that this book is stolen property. It was reported as "unsold and destroyed" to the publisher, and neither the author nor the publisher has received any payment for this "stripped book."

Recycling programs
for this product may
not exist in your area.

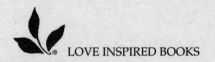

LOVE INSPIRED BOOKS

ISBN-13: 978-1-335-23190-1

Protecting His Secret Son

Copyright © 2019 by Laura Iding

All rights reserved. Except for use in any review, the reproduction or utilization of this work in whole or in part in any form by any electronic, mechanical or other means, now known or hereafter invented, including xerography, photocopying and recording, or in any information storage or retrieval system, is forbidden without the written permission of the editorial office, Love Inspired Books, 195 Broadway, New York, NY 10007 U.S.A.

This is a work of fiction. Names, characters, places and incidents are either the product of the author's imagination or are used fictitiously, and any resemblance to actual persons, living or dead, business establishments, events or locales is entirely coincidental.

This edition published by arrangement with Love Inspired Books.

® and TM are trademarks of Love Inspired Books, used under license. Trademarks indicated with ® are registered in the United States Patent and Trademark Office, the Canadian Intellectual Property Office and in other countries.

www.Harlequin.com

Printed in U.S.A.

Lead me in thy truth, and teach me: for thou art the
God of my salvation; on thee do I wait all the day.
—Psalms 25:5

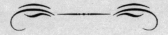

This book is dedicated to my son, Jonathan Iding,
who has followed in my footsteps to become
a registered nurse. I'm so proud of you!

ONE

Private investigator Mike Callahan scrunched down in the driver's seat of his black SUV and watched the front door of Duncan O'Hare's house through the open driver's-side window. He was parked in the driveway next door, knowing the young couple was out of town for the weekend. Duncan O'Hare was a Milwaukee cop, but Mike didn't believe the guy was dedicated to upholding the law.

Quite the opposite.

However, witnessing a meeting between Duncan O'Hare and Lane Walters, believed leader of the Dark Knights, two days ago outside an apartment building owned by Walters, wasn't enough. He needed proof to back up his suspicions. Mike had tailed Duncan, but the cop had managed to evade him.

On a mission to solve his father Max Callahan's murder, Mike wasn't about to let anything stand in his way.

His father had been shot in the back while visiting the crime scene of an officer-involved shooting. Four years later and the crime remained unsolved.

The key was buried deep within the Dark Knights, a civilian vigilante group known for meting out its own brand of justice against alleged criminals. There were several unsolved murders that were believed to be the work of the Dark Knights. As the police chief, his father had vowed to bring the Dark Knights down. Yet Mike knew the group had connections within the police force—possibly to Duncan O'Hare and Duncan's father, Ian O'Hare, who had conveniently taken Mike's father's place as chief of police after his death.

The night of his father's funeral, Mike had overheard a conversation between Ian and Duncan O'Hare about how much they secretly admired the Dark Knights. Mike's theory was that his father had learned about their connection to the vigilantes and had been murdered because of it. Mike wanted them arrested and held accountable for the role they'd played in his father's death. Staking out Duncan's house tonight had been a recent attempt to confront the cop about his meeting with Walters.

Duncan's front door unexpectedly opened and a pretty blonde stepped outside, holding the hand of a small boy who, in Mike's estimation, was around four or five years old. In the balmy May evening, there was plenty of light in the sky to see them clearly. The woman was wearing jeans and a pink hoodie with a white T-shirt underneath. He gasped and abruptly straightened as he recognized her.

Shayla O'Hare. Duncan's younger sister and Mike's former fiancée. He hadn't seen Shayla in four years, since their heated argument and breakup over her family's complicity in his father's murder. The child was a surprise. Since she hadn't had any children while they were together, Mike assumed the boy was a stepson or an adopted son. He ignored the shaft of pain to his heart at the thought of her being married to another man. She paused near the Jeep and leaned over to talk to the boy.

Out of the corner of his eye he noticed a dark sports car with tinted windows rolling down the street toward the O'Hare house. A tingling sense of danger had him tugging his gun from his shoulder holster.

The low-slung car slowed and he watched in horror as the passenger's-side window silently slid down, revealing the barrel of a gun. From what he could tell, the weapon was pointed directly at Shayla.

"Get down!" he shouted as he instinctively fired at the car in an attempt to save Shayla and the boy. The gunshot was loud, hitting the frame of the car with a metallic thud. Shayla screamed and he hoped and prayed she hadn't been hurt. He fired again, then shifted the gun to his left hand so he could push the start button. The SUV's engine roared to life.

The sports car accelerated and Mike yanked the gearshift into Drive. He stomped on the gas, gunning down the driveway toward the sports car. He attempted to ram his larger SUV into the small vehicle to halt its escape, but only clipped the back fender. The sports car fishtailed for a moment, then sped off.

He considered following it, but knowing that Shayla and a young boy were in danger had him twisting the wheel to pull in behind the Jeep. He hastily shut down the engine and jumped out, pausing for a moment to holster the gun.

"Shay? It's Mike Callahan. Are you and the boy all right?"

"Mike?" Her voice was faint and he approached cautiously, unwilling to scare them. "What's going on?"

Shayla and the child were huddled together behind the Jeep, smartly using the bulky frame as cover. The boy was crying, his faced pressed against Shayla.

"Are either of you hurt?" he asked, dropping down on one knee. "He's not crying because he's hit, is he?"

"N-no, we're fine. Just scared." Her pale, frightened

face belied her words. "Brodie, it's okay. We're safe now. You don't have to be afraid."

The little boy's sobs faded and he turned his tear-streaked face to look at Mike. "Is he a good guy, Mommy?"

Mike did his best not to flinch at hearing the word *mommy*. Shayla had broken his heart four years ago; he should be over their breakup by now.

"I—um, yes. He's a good guy." Her voice sounded thick as if she were on the verge of tears, as well.

He couldn't blame her. That had been a seriously close call. He wasn't surprised someone had come to Duncan O'Hare's house with a gun, although he didn't understand why Shayla and her son would be a target. "Come on, we need to get you both out of here before they decide to return."

"They who?" she asked. "I heard gunfire and caught a glimpse of the sports car driving away, but who was behind the wheel?"

"I don't know." He stared at her, amazed at how she was still so heart-wrenchingly beautiful. "I was hoping you could tell me."

She dropped her gaze and hugged the boy close. "I have no idea. I've only been back in Milwaukee for a couple of days."

Ignoring the urge to dredge up the past, he glanced at the Jeep. It must have belonged to her because Duncan drove a white pickup. "Let's go. We'll take my car."

"Wait." Shayla frowned. "Shouldn't we call the police?"

"My first priority is to get you and Brodie somewhere safe. We'll work out the rest later."

"O-okay." Shayla still looked a bit rattled but slowly rose to her feet. Brodie clung to her, so she hauled him up and into her arms. The kid was husky, no doubt about it. Smaller than Mike's seven-year-old niece, Abby, but not by much. "Will you get the child safety seat out of the Jeep?"

"Sure." He wrenched open the door and, thanks to practice with his abundance of nieces and nephews, expertly unlatched the seat and carried it to his SUV.

Five minutes later they were on the road, putting distance between them and the scene of the crime. If he hadn't been there, watching and waiting for Duncan to show... He shuddered. It was too easy to imagine the worst.

The attempt to kill Shayla and her son had to be related to Duncan's illegal activities. Unless there was something going on in Shayla's life that had placed her in danger.

"What brings you back to Milwaukee?" he asked, breaking the long silence.

Shayla didn't answer for a moment, glancing surreptitiously over her shoulder at the child tucked into the back seat. "I came to visit my father. He's in the hospital. In fact, that's where I was headed just now."

He inwardly winced. As much as he held her father and brother responsible for his father's death, he felt bad for what she was going through. "Is he going to be okay?"

She bit her lip and shrugged, avoiding his gaze. "He needs open-heart surgery. And you can stop pretending you care about my father's health. We both know that's a lie."

The bitterness in her tone reminded him of their last, horrible argument a few months after their breakup. Shayla had reached out to him, but he'd shut her down, unwilling to let go of his beliefs about her family's guilt. She'd accused him of being obsessed, and maybe he was.

He held his tongue, realizing there was no point in antagonizing her.

"Where is your brother? At the hospital? Or back at the house?"

She hesitated. "I'm not sure. He was supposed to meet me at the house for dinner, but didn't."

"Call him," he suggested.

"I did. Twice. It goes straight to voice mail."

"What time was he supposed to meet you?"

"We spoke to the doctor about Dad's surgery at eleven a.m. We both left the hospital then and were supposed to meet up again at three p.m., but Duncan never showed. I thought for sure he'd meet me at the house at five thirty for dinner, as planned. But he didn't do that, either."

Had Duncan realized Mike was following him? Mike glanced at the clock on his dashboard, noting it was almost seven o'clock. Seven hours wasn't a long time to be missing, but considering what he knew about Duncan's recent activities, he figured the guy may have got himself into trouble. Either that, or he was hiding from Mike.

"Do you know where Duncan likes to hang out?" he asked, hoping for a kernel of information he could use to find the guy.

"How would I know something like that?" Her voice shimmered with exasperation. "I live in Nashville, Tennessee. I'm only here because of Dad's hospitalization and upcoming surgery."

"Does your husband know you're here?" The blunt question popped out of his mouth before he could stop it.

"I'm not married, and my personal life is none of your business." She crossed her arms over her chest in a familiar, defensive move. "Where are we going?"

Shocked to hear she wasn't married, he didn't answer right away. His thoughts whirled and he wanted to know more about what Shayla had been doing over the past four years.

Mike forced himself to stay on task, keeping his eyes on the highway as he inwardly debated where to take Shayla and her son. No way would she agree to go to his place, and that seemed too personal anyway, so a motel was their best bet.

"I'm going to put you and Brodie up in a motel for the night." He took the exit ramp that would take him to the American Lodge Motel. The place was owned by a former firefighter and friend of his brother Mitch's. Their entire law enforcement family had used the motel as a safe haven while on the run from bad guys so often that they'd joked about renaming it the Callahan Lodge.

Now it was his turn to use it as a place to hide Shayla and her son. And he finally understood a little of what his brothers and his sister had gone through when they'd been in danger.

"Okay," she agreed. "Thank you."

The fact that she didn't argue was concerning. He couldn't help but wonder if she was keeping information from him.

"Shay, I need you to be honest with me. Is there anyone who wants to hurt you or the boy? Are you running from his father?"

"What?" Her eyes widened in horror. "No! Of course not."

"Then what's going on?"

"I don't know!" The denial was spit out through clenched teeth.

"Is this related to Duncan?" he pressed. "It's hard to understand why he wouldn't have met with you, considering your dad's upcoming surgery."

"He's a cop. I'm sure he had a good reason."

Her continued support of her brother grated on his nerves. He knew Duncan was up to his eyeballs in the

Dark Knights' illegal activities. And that involvement must have put Shayla in harm's way.

As much as he wanted to find out the truth about his father's murder, keeping Shayla and her son safe had to be his top priority.

Shayla twisted her hands in her lap, hoping Mike wouldn't notice how badly she was trembling.

Of all the men to come to her and Brodie's rescue, why did it have to be Michael Callahan?

Seeing him so unexpectedly after four years had sent her into an emotional tailspin. In some ways he looked the same—his dark hair worn long and shaggy, muscular build and brilliant green eyes. Dressed in black from head to toe had made him appear sinister at first, until he'd rushed to her rescue, his fear and worry for her and Brodie clear in his facial expression and tone.

She hadn't expected to see him again, although after visiting her father, noting his pale face and weakness while lying in his hospital bed, she'd decided to get in touch with Mike while she was in town. In fact, she was surprised he hadn't asked her a whole bucketful of personal questions.

Especially about Brodie.

Memories of the past, echoes of what might have been, overwhelmed her with sorrow and regret.

The man she'd fallen in love with and had agreed to marry, had changed after his father's murder. Mike had instantly become obsessed with uncovering the truth and had irrationally chosen to believe her father and brother were involved.

Ridiculous allegations had caused a terrible argument to erupt between them. Their breakup had been razor-sharp and deeply painful.

When she'd tried to call Mike several months later, he'd refused to talk to her unless she admitted her father and brother were guilty. When she'd refused, Mike had rudely told her they had nothing more to discuss.

So she'd let it go.

Yet, as time had worn on, she'd known she couldn't hide the truth forever. Her family knew and it was time for Mike to know, as well.

Tonight, she inwardly promised. She'd tell him tonight.

Mike drove up to a white two-story building called the American Lodge Motel. "Stay here," he said curtly. "I'll be right back."

Tempted to snap back, she bit her lip, knowing she should be grateful for Mike's timely rescue and ongoing support. After hearing the sharp report of gunfire and fearing for her life and Brodie's, the last thing she wanted to do was to spend the night at Duncan's.

The shooter had come to Duncan's house. Why? A shot meant for him? Not logical, since her fair hair was the opposite of his dark brown.

And where was Duncan? What was going on?

Her brother was a cop and she knew that often meant being called in to work after hours. But why wasn't he taking her calls? Why were they going straight to voice mail?

Questions only Duncan could answer.

She also couldn't figure out why Mike had been on the scene of the shooting so quickly. Was it possible he'd actually bought the house next to her brother's? No, that seemed highly unlikely. Four years ago, Mike had made his feelings for her brother crystal clear and she had no reason to doubt that anything had changed over time.

But she had seen Mike going down the driveway into the street in an attempt to hit the car speeding away.

She shot a guilty glance back at Brodie, whose brown

eyes were drooping sleepily despite the early-evening hour of seven thirty. No doubt, the poor kid was tuckered out between visiting his grandfather in the hospital and the most recent scare.

The driver's door opened, startling her. She put a hand over her galloping heart for a moment, then went back to twisting her fingers in her lap. "Find a room?"

"Two connecting rooms," he corrected. He started the car, made a sweep of the small parking lot and pulled up in front of room number nine. "We have nine and ten."

"We?" She hated the betraying squeak of alarm in her voice. "Why would you stay here, too?"

"Because you and the kid are both in danger, or has that fact not sunk in yet?"

She bit back a terse retort, unwilling to argue with him in front of Brodie. Yes, she knew she was in danger, but she didn't understand why.

She battled the surge of panic. She and Brodie were safe now, and she could handle Mike. He was just a man she'd once loved, but that was before he'd accused her father and brother of being dirty cops.

Pushing open her door, she slid out and then opened the back door to reach Brodie.

"Mommy?" His chubby fists rubbed his eyes. "Where are we?"

"We're staying overnight in a motel. Doesn't that sound like fun?" She unbuckled the straps holding him in and lifted him out of the seat with a muffled groan. Her son was big for his age, growing out of his clothes faster than she could buy them.

"Can we go swimming?" Brodie asked.

"I don't think so. But there's probably a kid's channel on the television." She set him on his feet. He was quick and prone to rushing off, so she firmly grasped his hand and then eyed Mike. "Which room is mine?"

"Number ten." Mike handed over a plastic keycard. "But I'd like you to keep the connecting door between our rooms open, in case things go south."

That was the last thing she wanted to do.

Silently, she took the key and slid it into the door, unlocking it. She stepped over the threshold and felt along the wall for a light switch.

A pale yellow glow filled the room, revealing two double-size beds, a small table and two wooden chairs. A waist-high dresser ran the length of the room with a medium-size television sitting on top of it. The space was larger than she'd anticipated and nicer, as if it had been recently updated. She urged Brodie inside, frowning when Mike followed.

"Hey," she protested when he crossed over to unlock her side of the connecting doors.

"I need to be able to reach you if there's any trouble," he repeated without showing signs of impatience. "I promise not to infringe on your privacy."

Once again, he was probably right, but his tendency to issue orders—as if he were a drill sergeant and she were a lowly soldier—didn't sit well. She'd forgotten how bossy he could be.

Except four years ago he hadn't been as prone to barking orders.

He'd been sweet, kind and caring…devastated after the fight with his father over turning down a position with the Milwaukee Police Department after graduating from the academy.

"What else are you not telling me?" he asked, breaking into her thoughts.

"Nothing!" She hoped her cheeks weren't flush with

guilt. "I don't know where Duncan is or where he normally hangs out." She turned on the television to help keep Brodie occupied. "Why don't you tell me why you were so Johnny-on-the-spot, parked next to Duncan's house in the first place?"

There was a brief flash of guilt in his green eyes but his expression remained impassive. "I was waiting for your brother."

The blunt answer surprised her. "Why?"

"To confront him about his illegal activities."

She narrowed her eyes. "Same song and dance, Mike? Aren't you tired of it yet?" She waved a hand and turned away. "Never mind. As you so rudely put it the last time we spoke, there's nothing more to discuss."

"Shayla, someone tried to shoot you outside Duncan's house. Doesn't that tell you something? Your brother's in trouble."

"The shot was aimed at me, not my brother. And did it ever occur to you that Duncan could be working undercover? That he's in danger because of a case he's working on? That maybe the attempt on me was a way to seek revenge against him?"

Mike didn't say anything for a long moment. "Anything is possible." The way he said it didn't give her the impression he really believed it. He moved toward the door. "I need to make a few calls, but holler if you need something, okay?"

Ironically, despite her irritation over the connecting doors between their rooms, she suddenly didn't want him to leave. "Mike?"

"Yeah?" He paused and looked at her over his shoulder.

The words were right there on the tip of her tongue, but she couldn't do it. Not yet. Not like this. She needed to wait until her son was asleep before uttering a deep, emotional confession. Her stomach rolled and she forced a smile. "Never mind. Good night."

He stared at her for a long moment before giving her a nod. "Good night."

He left, softly closing the door behind him. Her knees were shaky and weak, so she sank onto the edge of the bed and buried her face in her hands.

How was it possible he didn't know, or suspect, that Brodie was his son?

TWO

Mike's first call was to his buddy Hawk Jacobson. Hawk was another private investigator, and while they both preferred working alone, they also helped each other out on occasion.

"What?" Hawk answered.

"I need help."

"Again?" Hawk's tone was dry.

"Yeah, I know. Don't worry, I'll return the favor."

"Except that I don't get into trouble the way your family tends to."

Difficult to argue that one. Each of his siblings had a career in some kind of law enforcement and had been in danger more times than he could count over the past few years. Hawk's assistance had been instrumental in proving his brother's innocence when Mitch had been framed for murder last year.

"I heard Duncan O'Hare hasn't been seen since noon. It's too early to file a missing-persons report, but I have reason to believe he's in trouble. Any chance you can find out more? He has a partner, doesn't he? A guy named Peter Fresno?"

Mike could hear the sound of fingers tapping on a keyboard. "Yeah," Hawk agreed. "Peter Fresno is O'Hare's partner, working out of the fifth district."

"I need to talk to him."

Hawk snorted. "Good luck. Getting the address of a cop is nearly impossible. They protect that information closer than Fort Knox protects gold."

"Not if I can find another cop to provide that info to me." Mike had two brothers and a brother-in-law who were all Milwaukee cops. He didn't like asking them to break their code of ethics, but the lives of an innocent woman and her son were on the line. In his opinion, that trumped work ethics. "Anything you can find out would be helpful."

"Okay." Hawk disconnected from the line.

Mike sat for a moment, staring at his phone, debating who to call. His brother Miles was a homicide investigator. His brother Matt was a K-9 officer and his sister Maddy's husband, Noah, had just taken his detective exam, earning himself a gold shield.

May as well start at the top, he thought, scrolling through his contact list to find Miles. His brother answered almost immediately. "What's up?"

Mike sighed. "I guess it's my turn to need assistance."

"Hey, man, don't take it so hard. It was only a matter of time," Miles said in a consoling tone.

Mike couldn't help but chuckle. Hawk was right—the Callahans did have a way of getting into the middle of danger. "It's not really me, but a friend. A woman and her son."

"Really?" Miles's voice rose with interest. "Tell me more."

Mike rolled his eyes. Now that all the other Callahans were married and having kids, he was the only single guy left. A fact his family never let him forget. "Knock it off. I was keeping an eye on a suspect's house when I witnessed an attempt to kill a woman and her child. I was able to prevent that from happening and am now keeping her safe."

"Did you report it?" Miles asked.

"I'm reporting it to you right now. Because I trust you, Miles." And he didn't trust all of the cops on the force. "Unfortunately the car involved in the drive-by shooting took off and I didn't get a plate number. There may be shells or bullet fragments on the scene, so you need to send a few uniforms over to Duncan O'Hare's house to check it out."

"O'Hare?" Miles voice rose sharply. "The son of the police chief? That O'Hare?"

"Yeah. And his daughter, Shayla, was the intended victim."

Miles whistled. "This has to go straight to the top, Mike."

Exactly what he was trying to avoid. "You do what you need to do. But I'm working the case my way, and there's a guy I need to talk to. Peter Fresno. He's an MPD cop working out of the fifth district. I need his contact information, address and phone number."

There was a long silence on the other end of the line. Mike knew he was asking a lot and if Miles couldn't, or wouldn't, help him, he wasn't so sure Matt or Noah would, either.

"I'll see what I can do," Miles finally said. "You think Duncan's partner is responsible for the shooting?"

"No, I don't. But he may have information that can help."

"You're skating on the edge here, bro. You used to date Shayla, didn't you? Are you sure you're not letting your emotions cloud your judgment?"

Maybe, he silently admitted. Shayla and Brodie were the true innocents in this mess. "Look, two days ago I witnessed a meeting between Duncan O'Hare and the alleged leader of the Dark Knights, Lane Walters. I'm telling you, O'Hare has crossed over to the dark side."

"The chief's son? A dirty cop? Seriously? You better have hard-core proof to back up an allegation like that."

"Exactly. Which is why I need your help." Mike paused and then added, "I've never asked you for this kind of favor before, Miles. You know how much I prefer to work alone. This is critical or I wouldn't ask now."

Miles let out a heavy sigh. "Okay, okay. I'll call you back in a few." Miles clicked off and Mike stared down at his phone once again.

The case was important but his thoughts kept returning to Shayla, the woman he'd once loved, and her son.

For a brief moment he'd thought the boy was his, but the math didn't add up. Four years ago, the night he'd left the academy and his father had practically disowned him, he'd turned his back on his faith and his family, seeking solace in Shayla's arms.

They'd been seeing each other for six months by then and, knowing they'd gone too far, Mike hadn't hesitated in asking her to marry him. He'd been ecstatic when she'd agreed. They'd secretly made plans to go to the courthouse, but a week later his father was murdered. Ian O'Hare had instantly been appointed interim and then permanent chief of police.

From that moment on, especially after he'd heard Duncan and Ian talking about secretly supporting the Dark Knights, Mike had become obsessed with learning the truth.

An obsession that had torn him and Shayla apart.

But there was no sense in rehashing the past. Keeping Shayla safe was his priority. Hearing that she wasn't running from the boy's father had been slightly reassuring. But he still thought it was strange that the guy had let her drive from Nashville to Milwaukee alone, especially knowing that her father was sick in the hospital. Shouldn't he be here, supporting her?

Unless the guy was already out of the picture? Divorce or death… He winced and inwardly shrugged. As Shayla pointed out, her personal life was none of his business.

He rose and crossed the room to listen intently at the connecting door. There was nothing unusual past the muted sounds of the television.

He was about to step over the threshold to question her more about Brodie's father when his phone buzzed and Hawk's name popped up on the screen.

"What did you find out?" Mike asked.

"Not much. Apparently, Duncan's been off work for a couple of days."

That made sense based on his father's upcoming surgery. "Anything else?"

"No squawking about illegal activity, if that's what you mean. But we wouldn't hear even if there was a hint of scandal. Cops don't like to advertise when one of their own might be dirty."

"True, especially not the police chief's son." The task he faced suddenly seemed insurmountable. He did his best to shake off the impending sense of doom. "Hawk, would you do something else for me?"

The PI heaved a loud sigh. "Now what?"

"Dig into the background of a woman named Shayla O'Hare and a four- or five-year-old boy named Brodie."

"The sister? Why?"

"She's in danger and claims she doesn't know why. Denies she's running from the boy's father, but I need to know what I'm dealing with."

"Why not?" Hawk once again abruptly disconnected. The guy didn't like to use words like *hello* or *goodbye*, but Mike was used to it.

His phone rang again. This time it was Miles. "That was fast," Mike said.

"Yeah, well it's my turn to put Adam to bed so I have to make this quick. I was able to get Pete's address and a cell number." Miles rattled off the information as Mike scribbled it down on the motel notepad with a stubby pencil.

"How is Adam? Sleeping through the night?"

"Most of the time, but he's teething again so it's a toss-up whether or not he will this week." Pride was evident in his brother's tone. Miles and his wife, Paige, had two kids—Abby, who was seven, and Adam, who'd just turned one. Rumor had it that Miles and Paige were trying for baby number three, which was unfathomable.

Just because Mike and his siblings came from a family of six kids didn't mean they each needed to have the same number of children. But try telling his brothers and sister that. It seemed the Callahans were determined to populate the city.

Except for him. After his relationship with Shayla had disintegrated beyond repair, he'd focused on nothing more than finding the man responsible for his father's murder.

Besides, he wasn't interested in opening himself up to being hurt like that again. Not after the way Shayla had shattered his heart.

"Oh, I almost forgot," Miles continued, breaking into his thoughts. "The cops were already out at Duncan's place, someone reported the sound of gunfire. But they haven't found much."

"Not even a bullet fragment? That seems unlikely."

"It's early in the investigation," Miles pointed out. "But you also need to know there's a report of a black SUV fleeing the scene. I'm sure that was you, right?"

"Yep."

"No license plate number, but you might want to consider changing your vehicle, just to be safe."

"Okay, thanks. I appreciate the intel."

There was a slight pause then, "Mike?"

"Yeah?"

"Is this about Dad's murder?"

He hesitated. "Honestly? I think so, but have no proof." *Yet.*

Another pause. "I need you to be careful, okay?" Miles finally said. "And don't forget we're here if you need us. After all, our motto is that family sticks together. Don't shut us out. We all want to find the truth behind Dad's murder."

"I know." Mike was touched by his brother's offer. His siblings knew he was a bit of a lone wolf, forging his own path in the world. Which was exactly why he and his father had got into that fateful argument a week before his murder. His father had railed at him for being selfish, for not giving back to the community. Mike had tried to explain that he'd changed his mind. That he didn't want to wait to become a detective—that he'd wanted to do that now. But his father hadn't listened. And rather than try to talk it through, Mike had walked away, turned his back on his family and his faith.

The last words he'd said to his father had been in anger. After the murder, Mike had been assailed by guilt, desperately wishing he'd taken the opportunity to tell his dad he was sorry. That he loved him.

Something that still bothered him every single day.

Months later, after he'd come back to his family and his faith, he'd prayed that his father knew that he was sorry for the way they'd parted that day.

And hoped his father would forgive him.

"Mike?" Miles's voice brought his attention back to the present.

"Yeah. Thanks, Miles. I won't forget."

"Later, then." Miles hung up, leaving Mike to wonder how he should approach the new information. He wanted nothing more than to head right over to talk to Peter Fresno, yet at the same time the idea that his SUV might have been seen leaving Duncan's house nagged at him.

It wouldn't be the first time he'd asked Hawk to swap rides. He could always use one of his undercover identities to rent a different vehicle, too. It wasn't illegal to have an alternate ID as long as he didn't commit a crime while using it. He debated between doing something tonight or waiting until the morning.

Normally he wouldn't hesitate, but he didn't want to disturb Shayla and her son. The chances that someone could have tracked him from Duncan's house to the American Lodge were slim to nonexistent. And if they had? There would be cops already knocking at the door.

Convinced they were safe for the moment, he slipped his phone back into his pocket. Feeling restless, he paced the small interior of the room. He wanted to go over to Shayla's room to grill her about Duncan, but knew she wasn't going to tell him anything more than she already had.

And maybe she truly didn't know anything more. Interesting to find out she lived in Nashville and had only returned because of her father's illness. No wonder their paths hadn't crossed in the past four years.

Mike doused the lights and stretched out on the bed fully dressed. Since he didn't have his file on his father's murder to review, he thought it best to get caught up on rest. Working eighteen-hour days and sleeping less than six hours per night had taken its toll.

He fell asleep almost immediately, only to be woken by a piercing scream. Bolting out of bed, he grabbed his gun from the bedside table and barreled through the connecting door into Shayla's room, his heart practically thumping out of his chest as he frantically scanned for an intruder.

All he saw was Shayla cuddling Brodie close, whispering reassurances to him. Mike's heart rate slowed and he lowered his weapon, gulping air as he realized there wasn't any danger.

"Is there something I can do?" he asked, approaching cautiously.

"Put the gun away," she whispered harshly. "You're scaring him!"

He didn't bother to point out the kid had screamed in terror before he'd come in with his gun. He tucked the weapon into the back of his waistband, then stood awkwardly for a moment. "Are you sure you're not running from his father?" he asked.

"I'm sure." Her tone was firm.

"Then why the nightmare?"

Her deep brown eyes narrowed. "Obviously the scene in my brother's driveway must have scared him more than I realized. Hearing gunfire would frighten any child."

The boy's dark hair was a stark contrast to Shayla's riot of blond curls. He'd noticed earlier, the kid's brown eyes were identical to hers, though; a fact that niggled at him.

He glanced around the room, then took a step back. "Let me know if you need anything else, okay?"

"I will." She continued rocking the boy, pressing kisses to the top of his head while rubbing her hand along his back.

Mike didn't leave, even though he knew he should. Several minutes ticked by before the boy relaxed against her, appearing to fall asleep. Satisfied the crisis was over, Mike turned away. But once again she stopped him.

"Wait, Mike. Will you stay for a few minutes?" Her voice was soft, as if she didn't want to disturb her son.

"Uh, sure." Surprised she asked, he pulled out a chair and sat. "What do you need?"

"I need—*we need*—to talk." The seriousness of her tone made him frown.

"About what?"

She didn't answer for a long moment, then finally met his gaze. "Brodie's father."

Shayla knew she couldn't live with herself if she continued with the charade a moment longer. Gingerly, she eased away from her son so that he was lying on the pillow. He snuggled against it for a moment but didn't wake up. She pulled the covers up over his shoulders and then slipped off the bed.

She felt terrible about Brodie's nightmare. She'd hoped her young son hadn't noticed the gun pointed in their direction by the small black car or that the sharp report he'd heard was from a gun.

But Brodie was smart and she'd failed to protect him from the grim reality of gunfire. Maybe she should demand Mike take her to her Jeep so she could drive back to Nashville. Brodie didn't deserve to be subjected to terrifying experiences like this.

Then again, what if the danger followed her? What if the person trying to seek revenge on Duncan wouldn't hesitate to take her and Brodie out to make a point?

"You are running from him," Mike said, interrupting her thoughts.

"No." She took a deep breath and let it out slowly. She

had no idea how to tell him. "Let's go into your room, so we don't wake Brodie."

"Fine."

She picked up her cell phone in case the hospital staff called and followed him through the connecting door.

"Who is he?" Mike asked.

She stared at him, realizing that once she told him the truth, her life and Brodie's would never be the same. She'd noticed Mike didn't wear a wedding ring, but not all men did. He could still be involved with someone. The knots in her belly tightened painfully but she told herself to grow a spine. She locked her fingers and lifted her chin. "You are."

His jaw dropped comically, and then anger flashed in his green eyes. "Don't play games. Brodie is what—four? Going on five?"

"He's three," she corrected swiftly. "His birthday is in February. Valentine's Day to be exact. And yes, he's big for his age. But I'm not playing games. Why would I? Brodie is your son."

His face went blank for a moment, then he leaped to his feet. "And you're just telling me now?"

"Shh, don't wake him up. And I tried to call you when I found out, remember how that went?" She could tell her tone was defensive and tried to bring it down a notch. "You didn't give me a chance to tell you."

"You should have called me again," he countered, but his voice lacked heat. He stood and paced the length of the room. "I can't believe it. Mine. Brodie is my son!"

"Our son." Her phone vibrated in her pocket and she quickly pulled it out. She expected the call to be from the hospital but her brother's name flashed on the screen. "This is Duncan," she said in relief.

"Put it on speaker," Mike demanded.

She frowned and shook her head, fearing her brother

wouldn't talk freely if he knew she wasn't alone. "Duncan? Where are you? Why didn't you meet me at the hospital?"

"How's Dad?" His voice was soft, as if he were someplace he couldn't talk.

"He's fine. His surgery is still planned for the day after tomorrow. They want to make sure his blood pressure is stable before they put him under anesthesia." She could feel Mike's gaze boring into her and did her best to ignore it. "Where are you? I was worried when you didn't come back to the house."

"Yeah, well, I picked up a tail so I thought it was best to stay away."

"Picked up a tail?" She glared at Mike, knowing he'd likely been the one following her brother. "Tell me where you are and I'll meet you."

She held her breath, waiting, hoping, praying. Then finally her brother admitted, "I'm in a motel in Jacksonville. A place called the Rustic Resort. But don't come here. It's late and Brodie's probably asleep. I'll catch up with you tomorrow."

"Duncan, listen to me. Someone took a shot at me and Brodie outside your house. We needed protection, so I'm here with Mike Callahan. We'll pick you up, okay? It's better if we work together on this."

"You were shot at? That's crazy! Listen, I have to go." Her brother abruptly ended the call.

"Duncan?" Feeling frantic, she hit the redial button on her phone.

The call went straight to voice mail. She dragged her gaze to Mike's. "He hung up. I don't understand what's going on."

"Where is he?" Mike demanded.

"In Jacksonville." She hesitated, then added, "I'm worried he's in trouble. He didn't say it in so many words, but that's the sense I get."

"That's why I wanted you to put the call on speaker." The sharp note in his voice ticked her off.

"Well, we don't always get what we want, do we?"

Tension shimmered between them for a long moment and this time Mike turned away, raking a hand through his hair. "Okay, fine. Let's go get him."

"Good idea." She jumped to her feet. "Let me get Brodie."

Mike stared at her and she could tell he was thinking about the fact that Brodie was his son. "No need to wake him up. Give me the name of the motel and I'll head over to get your brother. Better that you and Brodie stay here where it's safe."

"No." She wasn't in the mood for his drill sergeant persona. "We're going with you."

"Not happening," Mike said firmly.

"You don't know the name of the motel, but I do. Besides, I said Duncan might be in trouble, not that he was in danger. I'm the one who was shot at. Don't you think we should stick together?"

Mike looked torn, as if considering her point.

"Let's go," she said. "We're wasting time arguing about this."

It was clear he didn't like it, but he reluctantly nodded. She spun on her heel and went back into her room to pick up Brodie.

As she lifted her son into her arms, she hoped that Duncan and Mike could find a way to work together.

Her safety and Brodie's could very well depend on it.

THREE

Reeling from the news he was Brodie's father, Mike struggled to stay focused. Shayla's stubbornness frustrated him, but the more he thought about it, the more he realized she was right. They absolutely needed to stick together. And he'd rather have both Shayla and Brodie with him than alone in a motel room.

His anger toward her was redirected to himself. She had called him a few months after their fight and he'd interrupted whatever she'd been about to tell him.

Granted, it had never entered his wildest dreams she might confess she was pregnant. That the one night they'd shared had changed their lives forever.

If anyone should have called again, it was him.

Standing awkwardly near the SUV, he waited for Shayla to strap Brodie into his car seat. When she finished, he held the passenger door open for her and she shot him a curious look as she slid into the passenger seat. He went around to the driver's side and put the SUV in gear.

Neither one of them broke the silence for several long moments.

"Why did you move to Nashville?"

"Huh?" She looked confused, then shrugged and turned away. "My aunt Jean lives there. She offered to help with the baby."

"I would have helped with Brodie." The words shot out of his mouth before he could stop them. Seemed to be happening a lot lately.

Shayla shifted in her seat to face him. "You accused my father and brother of being criminals, remember?"

He couldn't deny it. And he'd apologize except that two days ago he'd witnessed her brother meeting with Lane Walters. And to his eye, they'd appeared very friendly.

More miles passed before he spoke again. "You're sure he said Jacksonville?"

"Yes." She shivered a bit in the cool night breeze. Once the sun went down, the warmth promising a hint of summer quickly evaporated. The pink hoodie she wore wasn't very thick.

He turned up the heat for her sake and Brodie's, then glanced at her. "I want to be a part of Brodie's life."

Shayla let out a harsh laugh. "I'm sure you do. However, has it occurred to you that the two people you're accusing of being criminals are Brodie's *uncle* and *grandfather*?"

A hard lump formed in the back of his throat, making it impossible to speak. She was right, he hadn't considered that fact, yet he couldn't let go of what he knew in his heart was true. Duncan and Ian were involved in his father's murder and needed to be brought to justice.

No matter the consequences? His resolve wavered. He couldn't lose his son.

"Yeah, that's what I thought," Shayla said in a weary tone. "You really won't even entertain the idea that Duncan is working undercover?"

"I'll consider it," he said, forcing the admission past his tight throat. "I'm willing to listen to your brother's side of the story."

"That's something, I guess." Shayla turned to stare out the passenger window.

He knew he needed to tread lightly from here on out. Alienating Shayla wouldn't help his goal of being involved in Brodie's life.

Maybe a mediator would help. He dug his phone out of his pocket and gently lobbed it over the center console. "Find Hawk's number—it's in my most recent calls. I spoke to him ten minutes ago. Wouldn't hurt to have backup."

She fumbled with the phone for a moment, then hit the number and the speaker. The sound of a ringing phone could be heard before a sleepy, querulous voice answered. "Callahan, don't you sleep?"

His mouth quirked in a reluctant smile. "I need backup, can you meet me in Jacksonville?"

Hawk uttered a low groan. "Yeah, but I need to know where exactly you want to meet."

"To a motel called…" He waited for Shayla to pipe in.

"The Rustic Resort," she finally admitted.

Hawk made some sort of grunting sound and then the line went silent.

"That was weird," Shayla murmured. "He didn't say goodbye."

"That's just how Hawk is." He held out his hand for the phone and she dropped it into his palm. The device was warm from her touch and he closed his fingers around it, wishing he could go back in time to do things differently.

"Mommy? I'm hungry."

Shayla reached behind her seat to lightly touch her son's knee. "We'll get something later, okay?"

"We can stop and get something," Mike interjected. He felt bad for not thinking of it sooner. He'd forgotten what it was like to be around little kids.

Not just any kid.

His son.

Her expression turned wry. "We picked up dinner at Burger Barn shortly before you came rushing to our rescue. Trust me, this is normal. Brodie's always hungry. The kid has an appetite that doesn't quit."

He found himself mesmerized by every morsel of information she doled out about his son and insatiable for more. He wanted to ask about everything from how her pregnancy went to the delivery to who watched Brodie while she worked, if she worked, which he assumed she must. It burned to know that he hadn't paid a dime of child support.

He would have, if he'd known. And whose fault was that?

His. And hers. But mostly his.

The sight of the Jacksonville sign interrupted his crazy thoughts. They'd made good time, arriving sooner than expected. "We need to find out where the Rustic Resort is located."

"It's off County Highway BB." She was looking down at her phone. "Roughly five miles from here."

He hoped Hawk had made good time as well, because he wasn't about to put Shayla or Brodie in danger. He and Hawk would talk to Duncan, while Shayla and Brodie stayed well out of the way.

"I think that's it, up ahead."

He saw the building she indicated and slowed down to pull off the road. Hitting the redial button on his phone, he called Hawk. "How far away are you?"

"Eight minutes, maybe less."

Sitting out in the open like this made him twitchy. It was past midnight, which meant traffic out here in no-man's-land was nonexistent. They were an obvious target and he didn't like it. "I'm going to drive past the place, see what we're dealing with. Call me when you get close."

"Yep."

He tucked his phone into his pocket and pulled back out onto the highway. The Rustic Resort was all rustic and very little resort, with ten rooms in a long row. It was set back about one hundred feet from the highway, but even as he drove past, he could see there were only three cars parked in the lot and none of them was a white pickup. A black pickup was in front of the third room, but not a white one, the kind Duncan drove.

A chill snaked down his spine.

Either Duncan had ditched his truck and hitched a ride, or he'd got his hands on a spare vehicle. For Shayla's brother's sake, he hoped it was the latter.

Without a ride handy, her brother would be stuck there like a mouse in a trap.

From what he could tell, the motel butted up against a farmer's field. There were long rows of newly turned dirt and a farmhouse way out in the distance. No lights were on inside the place, making him wonder where the owners of the land were. Or maybe they just leased the land to someone else who did the work.

Worst of all, the farmland didn't offer any type of cover. He couldn't imagine what Duncan was thinking to choose this place. He and his brothers would have looked for something with an escape route. Even the American Lodge had one, especially from the corner room that he'd given Shayla.

At the next intersection, he turned right and pulled off the road. He tapped his fingers on the steering wheel. Patience wasn't his strongest attribute and he was finding it difficult to wait on Hawk. After five minutes had passed, he pulled out his phone, but before he could call Hawk, his buddy's name popped up on the screen.

"I'm approaching the motel now," Hawk said without preamble. "What's the plan?"

"There isn't any coverage behind the place, so I'll park on the south end of the lot while you take the north. We'll meet in the middle."

"Know how many hostiles we're facing?"

"Nope. But I'm sure we'll find out soon enough." He hung up, hoping Shayla hadn't heard Hawk's term for her brother. Hawk had spent time as a soldier, fighting overseas in Iraq. In Hawk's world, anyone who wasn't a good guy was automatically deemed a hostile.

Despite seeing the meeting between Duncan and Lane, Mike couldn't help admitting Shayla had a point. There was a chance, albeit a remote one, that her brother was working undercover.

It didn't explain what he'd overheard at his father's funeral, but still. He'd promised to listen to Duncan's side of the story, and he would.

After making a U-turn, Mike headed back toward the motel. He could see Hawk's SUV headlights approaching from the opposite direction. Relieved to have Hawk's assistance, he pulled into the parking lot, turned around and backed into the spot near the south side of the building. He purposefully positioned the SUV so that it was directly facing the road, in case Shayla had to leave in a hurry.

"You need to get in behind the wheel," he directed. "And if anything goes wrong, I want you and Brodie to bolt out of here, understand?"

Her expression was full of concern. "And leave you? I don't think that's a good idea."

"I'll be fine with Hawk. You have our son to worry about."

She bit her lip, then nodded. "Okay. You'll be careful, right? You won't hurt Duncan?"

It was on the tip of his tongue to point out that he would only take action against Duncan if her brother started it first, but there was no reason to say anything that might upset her.

"Everything will be fine," he said reassuringly. "This is all just an added precaution. But promise me that if you hear anything go wrong, you'll drive straight to the closest police station. Ask for my brother Miles, or Matt. Or Noah Sinclair. And if all else fails, you can ask for my dad's buddy Kirk Stoltz."

Her expression held a note of uncertainty. "I will."

He hoped so. He slid out from behind the wheel. Shayla awkwardly climbed over the console and dropped into the driver's seat. He waited until she had the seat adjusted for her shorter frame before gently closing the door and loping across the parking lot to meet up with Hawk.

"Which room?" Hawk asked.

"I don't know. We could ask the clerk." He frowned when he noticed the black pickup. There was something off about it. "Wait a minute. I want to check this out."

"I'll cover you."

Next to his brothers and brother-in-law, Hawk was the only other person Mike trusted to cover his back. Despite being injured during his stint as a soldier, with a long jagged facial scar to prove it, he knew Hawk would go to the mat for him, and vice versa.

Mike hunkered down beside the truck and swept his hand over the side panel. It wasn't smooth, the way paint from a factory was. There were rough spots. He turned on his phone and used the flashlight application to inspect the underbelly.

Edges of white paint could be seen behind the black.

"This is Duncan's truck," he whispered. "He must have painted it black to disguise it. He's likely in room three."

"Not necessarily," Hawk pointed out.

Mike knew Hawk was right. He'd purposefully parked in front of his own room at the American Lodge, leaving the space in front of Shayla's room vacant. That way the room looked empty. If he were staying here, he'd absolutely park in a different spot. Especially with so many to choose from.

"We'll try three first." Using the truck for cover, he approached the motel door. He flattened himself against the wall on one side of the door, leaving Hawk to do the same on the other side.

He rapped on the door with his knuckles.

Nothing.

He and Hawk exchanged a long glance before he tried again with the same result.

They repeated the tactic on number two and number four.

Still no response.

"Let's check with the clerk," Mike finally said.

Hawk followed as they went inside the small lobby. An elderly man looked up in surprise. Judging by the bilateral hearing aids, the guy hadn't heard them knocking outside or their approach as they'd walked in.

Mike flashed smile. "I'm here to pick up a friend of mine, Duncan O'Hare. He called me from room three, but isn't answering the door."

"Eh?" The man leaned forward. "What's the name?"

"Duncan O'Hare," he repeated loudly. "Room three."

The old man used his two index fingers to tap on the computer screen, then sagely nodded. "Yes, he's here."

Mike glanced at Hawk and then repeated himself. "Duncan's not answering the door. He must be really sound asleep. Would you mind giving us a key? I don't want to wake up your other guests."

The guy frowned. "I don't know about that…"

Mike lifted his hands. "I get it, no problem. We'll just keep knocking, I'm sure he'll wake up eventually." Without hesitating, he turned and began to walk away.

Before he reached the door, the elderly man called him back. "Wait, son. Take the key."

The threat of creating a lot of noise had worked. Mike flashed a grateful smile. "Thanks, I appreciate it. Poor guy's going through a rough time."

"Aren't we all?" the old guy agreed. "Business ain't so good these days. Can't afford to lose my guests."

Key in hand, Mike approached the door cautiously. Hawk once again took up a defensive position on the other side of the door. Mike unlocked the door and pushed it open with his foot while hugging the wall.

Still nothing.

He and Hawk cautiously entered the room, noticing the fast-food wrappers in the garbage bin and that the bedspread was messed up, as if someone had stretched out there.

But there was no sign of Duncan O'Hare.

A feeling of helplessness washed over him. Duncan had left, without his white-painted-black truck.

Leaving nothing resembling a clue behind.

Waiting for Mike was sheer torture. Shayla gripped the steering wheel, hoping that he'd hurry up and get her brother out of the motel. She'd feel better if Duncan stayed with her, Brodie and Mike.

There was strength in numbers.

Mike and his friend Hawk moved with excruciating slowness. The wait was killing her. She wasn't cut out for this kind of thing. Skulking around in the dark was causing her imagination to run wild.

If this level of suspense continued, she was afraid Brodie wouldn't be the only one to suffer from nightmares. She'd have them, too.

Braced for the worst, she hunched her shoulders, listening intently for any sound of a struggle. She doubted Duncan would welcome Mike with open arms and prayed things wouldn't get out of hand.

Now that Mike knew the truth about Brodie, she couldn't help wondering how they'd make things work between them. Selfishly, she didn't want to share custody on alternate weekends and days of the week. Brodie didn't even know Mike—surely he wouldn't force the issue of custody right away.

And Mike's opinion about her father and brother still rankled.

When she saw the two men emerge from the motel room, her stomach knotted. The men parted ways. Mike returned to the SUV while his buddy Hawk walked to a different vehicle on the other side of the parking lot.

She belatedly scrambled back over the console into the passenger seat. As soon as Mike was settled, she peppered him with questions.

"What happened? Where's Duncan? Did you talk to him? Is he upset? Let me try…"

Mike started the engine, clicked his seat belt into place and turned to face her, his expression grim. "I'm sorry, Shay, but he's not there."

She narrowed her gaze. "You must have the wrong room."

"No, the guy at the front desk confirmed Duncan was staying in room three and that's his truck, now spray-painted black, parked out front. There are signs he was there, but he's gone now."

Her jaw dropped and she twisted to look through the back window. "You're sure?"

"Yeah, I'm sure." Mike drove out onto the highway, heading back the way they'd come.

"But—" She glanced back at Brodie, who'd nodded off while they'd waited for Mike. She didn't want her son to overhear her next question. "Do you think he's hurt? Was there any sign of a struggle? Like—blood?"

"No sign of trouble," he assured her, reaching over to give her hand a reassuring squeeze. It was the first time he'd voluntarily touched her and she was shocked by the tingling sensation that skipped along her nerve endings. She had to remind herself this wasn't the time for long-dormant hormones to run amok. "Try not to think the worst, okay?"

She nodded, because speaking past the lump in her throat wasn't an option. Losing Duncan would be awful. He'd been the main point of contact with her family. Her father had been upset about her pregnancy at first but had eventually come around. But being police chief took a lot of his time. Since her mother had died when she and Duncan were young, Aunt Jean had stepped in to help raise them. Once they were grown, Aunt Jean had moved to Nashville. Joining her aunt in Tennessee had been Shayla's choice.

Aunt Jean, Duncan and her father were her only supporters.

Where was her brother? What in the world was going on?

"He's working undercover," she repeated, more to convince herself than anything else. Mike might claim her brother was involved in something illegal but she refused to believe it. "He knew I was safe with you, so he decided to go off on his own to work the case."

"It's possible," Mike agreed. "Do you want me to pick up something for Brodie to eat?"

"Huh? Oh, no. He should be fine until morning. I have fish crackers in my purse if he needs something."

"I don't mind," he insisted. "Just let me know."

"Duncan didn't leave a note or anything?"

"Not that I saw." Mike glanced at her. "Try his cell again."

She did, but naturally her brother didn't pick up. She hadn't expected him to.

"I'm worried," she confessed softly. "I don't understand where Duncan would go without his truck. This place is too far out to get anywhere on foot. It just doesn't make any sense."

"Hold that thought." Mike's gaze was focused on the rearview mirror. "We have company."

"What?" She twisted in her seat, her heart skittering at the bright headlights growing larger and closer behind them. "It's probably Hawk."

"It's not. Hawk took a different route. Besides, these headlights are low and widely spaced, like a sports car. They're not high enough to be an SUV."

Remembering the sports car that had pulled up in front of Duncan's house caused fear to rake like talons along the back of her neck. Peering over her shoulder, she glanced at her sleeping son. "What are we going to do?"

"Lose them. Hang on." That was all the warning he gave her before yanking the wheel hard to the left. The SUV bounced wildly as he drove toward a farmer's field. She gripped the armrest, digging her fingernails into the cushion.

Brodie woke up and began to cry, no doubt because of the rough ride.

"It's okay, Brodie, we're fine. Don't be afraid."

Brodie continued to cry and she wanted to beg Mike to get them out of the field as soon as possible. She kept reassuring Brodie but his cries grew louder and louder.

She craned her neck, trying to see where the headlights were, when the sound of gunfire echoed through the night.

Someone in the car behind them was shooting at them!

FOUR

Clank! They'd been hit!

"Keep your head down," he ordered, the sound of a bullet hitting metal sending Mike's pulse rocketing into triple digits. Wrenching the steering wheel to the side, he abruptly pulled off the road and headed directly into the deeply rutted and newly plowed field. Unable to bear the thought of Shayla or Brodie being injured by a bullet, he earnestly began to pray.

Heavenly Father, please keep Shayla and our son safe in Your care!

The wheel jerked in his hands and he did his best to put more distance between him and the gunmen in the sports car.

"Where are you going?" Shayla asked shakily as Brodie's crying intensified. The SUV rolled from side to side as Mike pushed the vehicle as fast as he dared over the uneven terrain.

"Our goal is to reach the old farmhouse up ahead." His fingers gripped the steering wheel tightly. "I doubt the sports car will be able to follow us."

"Are you crazy?" Shayla twisted in her seat while keeping her head low.

He risked a glance at his rearview mirror. "They'll bottom out and get stuck if they try."

True enough, the sports car pulled off the road, then ground to a halt.

"What if they come after us on foot?"

He loosened his grip enough to reach for his phone. He tossed it into her lap. "Call Hawk, tell him to come back this way."

Brodie's crying had subsided to hiccuping sobs that tore at his heart. Mike wanted nothing more than to pull his son into his arms and comfort him. Impossible not only because he was driving, but he was also nothing more than a stranger to the little boy.

Shayla's voice was shaky as she explained their tenuous situation to Hawk. Mike was confident his PI buddy would instantly return to help them out.

He prayed again, this time that Hawk would arrive before it was too late.

Glancing again at the rearview mirror, he searched for signs of the gunmen following on foot. He was armed, and an expert marksman, but one weapon against two or more wasn't reassuring.

His heart dropped to his stomach when he saw two dark figures get out of the sports car. Sick with fear, he pushed the SUV faster. Reaching the shelter of the farmhouse was their best chance of defending themselves. The field didn't offer any hiding places, but he was sure he'd be able to hold them off long enough for Hawk to arrive.

"They're coming," Shayla whispered in horror.

"We're going to be okay. God is watching over us." He did his best to sound positive.

Tiny headlights could be seen in the distance coming from the south and Mike hoped it was Hawk riding to the rescue. He couldn't see the dark shapes behind them any longer and couldn't say for sure if the two men were still advancing or had turned back.

He continued praying as the farmhouse grew larger. Up close, he could see it was in worse shape than anticipated. Several windows were broken and he thought there may be a few holes in the ceiling, but a dilapidated structure was better than nothing.

The SUV abruptly lurched to one side, his left front tire hitting a large rock. There was a loud noise, as if something underneath had broken. He shifted his weight toward his door, hoping the vehicle wouldn't tip over.

"Mike!" Shayla said with a gasp.

A second later the SUV landed on all four tires and he hit the brake, bringing the car to a stop. "We need to get inside. Hurry!"

Shayla had already unbuckled her seat belt and was pushing her door open, clearly frantic to get to their son. He pulled his weapon and hurried around the front of the car to help. She lifted Brodie into her arms, holding him protectively against her chest.

"We're going in around the back," Mike said, sweeping his gaze over the field. The black sports car was still there, but he couldn't make out whether or not the two gunmen were still on the loose.

The half-moon offered some light but he used his phone's flashlight app to illuminate the way inside the house. The back door wasn't locked and he hoped no one else was hiding inside.

He held his breath, sweeping the beam from his phone over the interior of the building.

It appeared to be empty. The inside smelled dank and musty, a thick layer of dust covering every surface. There were no recent footprints in the dust covering the floor and he winced when he saw mouse dirt.

"It's awful in here," Shayla whispered.

He couldn't disagree. "I know, but it's temporary until Hawk arrives."

Shayla didn't argue, though he could tell she wasn't about to put Brodie down anytime soon.

"Stay behind me," he instructed, moving through the structure to the part of the house overlooking the highway. He turned off his phone light and stood, waiting for his eyes to adjust to the darkness.

A few minutes later he could see enough to approach the dust-caked window.

The sports car was gone! Relief washed over him but then he realized that one of the gunmen could still be out there somewhere. That moving the sports car might be a ruse to lull him into complacency.

The lower corner of the window next to him was broken, so he made his way over and hunkered down to watch for signs of movement. The twin headlights he'd noticed earlier grew brighter as it approached, but he kept his gaze on the open stretch of field between the highway and the farmhouse.

"Shayla, have you heard of the Dark Knights?"

"No. Why?"

He shouldn't have been surprised; not only was she living in Nashville, but her brother likely wouldn't mention his association to them, either. Still, he had to know for certain. "You're sure Duncan didn't say anything about them?"

"Are you back to that again?" Shayla's voice was strained. "You should know better than anyone that Duncan would never mention anything related to his undercover work to me." There was a pause, then she added, "Do you think that's why he left the Rustic Resort? Because of this Dark Knights thing? What does that even mean?"

"It's a group of civilian vigilantes who take the law into their own hands to mete out justice when the legal system fails to work." He glanced back at her. "They've been known to kill people who they deem guilty of a crime. And worse, they have support within the police force."

She glared at him. "Don't go there," she warned.

He turned back to stare out at the field, acknowledging it wasn't the time or the place to interrogate her. The headlights were even brighter now and he felt sure it was Hawk coming to their rescue.

"Mommy, I'm hungry," Brodie said, breaking the strained silence.

He couldn't help but smile when he heard Shayla sigh. "Okay, have a few fish crackers."

Without taking his gaze off the field, Mike said, "Remind me to stop at the store tomorrow so we can stock up on crackers."

For a moment there was nothing but the sound of Brodie chewing and swallowing.

"Do you see anyone out there?" she asked.

"The sports car is gone. No sign of anyone on foot, either. This is Hawk coming to get us now."

The twin headlights turned toward the farmhouse as Hawk drove through the open field the same way Mike had done earlier. The headlights illuminated the area enough that Mike could see that no one else was out there.

Hawk's arrival must have scared the gunmen off. Mike stood, reholstered his gun and faced Shayla. "We can head outside now, they're gone."

"The bad guys are gone?" Brodie repeated, his mouth stained orange from the cheesy crackers.

"Yes, they're gone," Mike repeated, wishing once again he could pull his son into his arms. "You and your mom are safe with me."

The boy nodded and rested his head on Shayla's shoulder. "'Kay."

He turned on his phone flashlight again, illuminating the way through the rickety old farmhouse. They went back outside in time to see Hawk pulling in behind Mike's SUV.

"I saw them take off," Hawk said. "I wanted to follow, but knew I needed to come here. And I was too far away to get a license plate number." Then he let out a low whistle. "I see they hit your car."

Mike went over to see what Hawk was talking about. The bullet hole was located to the right of the back of the car.

The passenger side.

His stomach knotted with fear as he realized how close Brodie's car seat had come to being hit.

How close he'd come to losing the son he'd just discovered he had.

Shayla shifted Brodie into her arms, bracing the bulk of his weight on her hip. He was heavy and she hadn't wanted to put him down in the grimy farmhouse.

Her phone buzzed in her purse and she fished around for it. Her heart quickened when she recognized the number for the hospital.

"Hello?" she quickly answered.

"Ms. O'Hare? This is Dr. Torres."

"What's wrong? Is my dad okay?" She couldn't imagine why her dad's surgeon would be calling her so late.

"Everything is fine," he said reassuringly. "In fact, he's doing so much better that I'd like to move up his surgery to first thing tomorrow morning."

"So soon?" She couldn't decide if this was good news

or bad. "But—I thought you were worried about his blood pressure."

"He's been stable all day and I think it's best we get in to replace his cardiac arteries as soon as possible."

She couldn't help glancing at Mike, who'd come over to stand beside her. Despite being at odds earlier, she appreciated his support now. "Okay, thanks. I appreciate the call."

"He's scheduled for first thing in the morning," Dr. Torres went on. "And I expect he'll be back in his room in the cardiac intensive care unit by noon if you want to visit."

"I'll be there." She wanted to be there early to see her dad off, but wasn't sure that was feasible. "Can I talk to my dad?"

"Of course. I'll have the nurse transfer this call into his room." There was another long pause, then more ringing.

"Hello?" Her dad's hoarse voice made her eyes sting with tears.

"Hi, Dad. It's Shayla. I hear you're having surgery tomorrow morning."

"Yep, that's the plan. How are you and Brodie doing? I thought you were coming back here tonight."

Unwilling to add to her father's stress level, she decided against telling him about the episodes of gunfire. "Brodie's being fussy, so we'll come in tomorrow, okay? I'll see you after surgery."

"Sounds good." Was it her imagination or did her father's voice sound weaker? "I'll look forward to seeing you, Brodie and Duncan tomorrow, then."

"I'll be there," she promised, feeling sick at the thought it was likely Duncan wouldn't be. "I love you, Dad. Get better soon."

"I will. Hug my grandson for me."

"Done. Good night." She disconnected, feeling awful about not being there for her dad. She closed her eyes and dropped her chin to rest on Brodie's head. What if something happened and he didn't survive his surgery?

"He'll be all right," Mike said in a low voice. "We'll pray for him."

She hadn't grown up with God and faith the way the Callahans had. But she nodded. "I'd like that."

"Okay." Mike put his hand on her back and bowed his head. "Dear Lord, we ask that You keep Ian O'Hare safe in Your care as he undergoes surgery at Trinity Medical Center. Amen."

"Amen," she whispered. It felt weird to pray out loud, with Mike standing beside her, but she couldn't deny feeling a little better afterward. "Thanks, Mike."

"Anytime." He hesitated and then added, "Listen, Shayla, I'd like you to get rid of your phone. I'm worried that the gunmen may be using it to track your movements."

"What?" Her head snapped up, all sense of peace instantly vaporized. "I can't do that. This is the only number the hospital has to reach me."

"It's okay, we'll give them my number so that we'll still be accessible." He gently pried her phone from her hand. "Trust me on this, okay? These devices have GPS tracking imbedded inside. We can't risk the possibility of being found."

"Mike's right about that," Hawk piped up. "Best to smash it to pieces and leave it behind."

Her brain told her they were right, but her heart wanted to rail at Mike for taking away the meager connection she had to her father.

And to her brother. Without her phone, Duncan wouldn't have any way to contact her if he needed to be rescued.

"Shayla? Please?"

She let out a heavy sigh. "What's your number? I want to call the hospital right now to make sure they have it."

He provided the information and she used his phone to make the call. She left his cell number with her dad's nurse and then called her dad's room again, to make sure he had it, as well. Her dad asked why she was with Mike, and she assured him they were just friends catching up. He seemed to accept her response. It occurred to her that Duncan might call the hospital, even her father, to find a way to reach her if her phone didn't work.

"Good night, Shayla."

"Good night, Dad." She sighed, handed the phone back to Mike and hitched Brodie up again, ignoring the screaming protest of her arm muscles.

"Do you want me to carry him?" Mike offered.

Despite her fatigue, she shook her head. "He doesn't know you. I don't want him to be afraid."

Mike's disappointment was palpable and she was reminded of the fact that, as Brodie's father, he was well within his rights to hold his son.

But not yet. Not until Brodie had a chance to get used to Mike.

"We'll swap rides," Hawk said, holding out his keys.

"No, driving my SUV will only put you in danger," Mike protested. "I'll grab Brodie's car seat and we'll go together."

Hawk frowned. "I'm not sure leaving your ride here is a good idea. They could come back to run the plates, find out who you are."

Shayla froze. "I don't like that idea."

"I'm not sure it's drivable, hitting the rock damaged the front axle. I'll arrange to have it towed," Mike assured her.

"Call now," Hawk advised. "You don't know how long it will take for the tow truck to get here."

Shayla leaned against the busted SUV in an attempt to disperse Brodie's weight. Mike called the tow truck, then took the car seat out and buckled it into Hawk's SUV.

"Ready?" Mike asked, looking at Shayla and then at Hawk.

She nodded and gratefully set Brodie into his car seat with a muffled groan. After making sure he was secure, she went around to slide into the seat beside him, leaving Mike to take the front passenger seat.

"Where to?" Hawk asked as he began the rocky drive through the farmer's field.

Mike didn't answer right away. "What do you think about us spending some time at your cabin?" he finally asked. "It's safer and closer than going back to the city."

"Good idea," Hawk agreed. "I was there last weekend, so there's plenty of supplies and nonperishable food."

A cabin? She hoped it was in better shape than the farmhouse had been.

"Don't worry, there's indoor plumbing," Hawk said as if reading her mind. He captured her gaze in the rearview mirror. "And it's relatively clean."

"Thank you," she said, feeling bad about her unkind thoughts. "I appreciate you helping us out."

"Yeah, the Callahans owe me big-time and I have every intention on finding a way to collect."

"I'm sure you will," Mike agreed dryly.

Brodie yawned, his head tilting to one side. His eyelids fluttered despite the jostling of the SUV as Hawk made his way through the field.

She put a reassuring hand on his legs to steady him during the rough ride. At least it wasn't as scary as running from the gunmen.

When they reached the road, Shayla finally relaxed in her seat, feeling safe for the first time in hours. On one hand, her father was doing well enough to have surgery. But on the other, Duncan was still missing.

The ride to Hawk's cabin took less than twenty minutes. His driveway wasn't paved, but wasn't nearly as bad as driving through the field had been.

"Give us a minute while we get the lights," Mike said.

She nodded, battling a wave of exhaustion. Hopefully, Brodie wouldn't wake up when she carried him inside.

When the lights went on in the cabin, she pushed open her door and slid out. She walked around to the other side so she could unbuckle Brodie.

"Shay?" Mike's voice was soft and husky beside her. "Will you allow me to carry him inside?"

She hesitated but then nodded, taking a step back to give him room. Mike slid his broad hands beneath Brodie and carefully lifted him out of the seat, cradling him against his chest.

Their son wiggled around a bit but didn't wake up.

Mike surprised her by pressing a kiss to Brodie's temple as he carried him inside the cabin. Her heart fluttered at the picture they made together, father and son, both having the same dark hair, with the cowlick that refused to lie flat.

This was it, she thought, shivering as she followed them inside. The point where life as she'd previously known it ended and a new life full of unknowns began.

From this moment on, she'd have to share Brodie with his father.

FIVE

Mike cradled his precious son for a moment, inhaling Brodie's baby-shampoo scent as Shayla opened a sleeping bag on one of the twin beds in Hawk's guest room. His heart swelled with love and longing. Holding his son in his arms felt amazing and he was loath to let him go.

Shayla finished with the sleeping bag and stepped back, eyeing him expectantly. Obviously he couldn't stand there with Brodie all night, so he gently and reluctantly placed Brodie on the bed. He lightly covered Brodie's husky frame with the edge of the sleeping bag and then bent to press a kiss on the top of the boy's head.

"Good night, son," he whispered.

Shayla ducked her head, avoiding his gaze as she straightened the edge of the sleeping bag. She also kissed Brodie, then picked up a chair and set it back-first against the bed.

"What's the chair for?" he asked after they tiptoed out of the room.

"He has a big-boy bed at home, but there's a safety rail along the side to make sure he doesn't roll out onto the floor." Shayla crossed her arms over her chest and looked past him at the kitchen. "I figured the back of the chair should work just as well."

"I see." He felt foolish for not knowing more about how to take care of a three-year-old. It never occurred to him that the boy could roll off the bed onto the floor. "Good idea."

"Where's Hawk?"

"He left, but will be back in the morning with another vehicle, a laptop computer and a set of disposable phones." He sensed she was uncomfortable with him, but didn't quite understand why. "Are you hungry? You want something to eat? I was hoping we could talk for a bit. I have so many questions about your pregnancy, Brodie's delivery and your childcare arrangements…"

"No, I'm fine. Except I'm not really up for a conversation. If you don't mind, I'd rather try to get some sleep, especially since it's likely Brodie will have another nightmare."

"But—" He swallowed his protest, hating to admit she was right. They'd narrowly escaped another round with the gunmen and he had no idea what impact their rugged escape through the farmer's field would have on Brodie. "Okay, see you in the morning."

"Good night." Shayla went into Brodie's room, quietly shutting the door behind her.

Mike let out his breath in a heavy sigh and went into the kitchen. Hawk was right about there being plenty of food, even instant oatmeal for breakfast. Did Brodie like instant oatmeal?

He had no idea.

There were many unknowns. So many things he wanted to know. Details that Shayla was apparently unwilling to share.

He went into the living room and stretched out on the sofa. His weapon dug into his side, but he didn't want to set it on the table, on the chance Brodie would wake and wander into the living room. Just the image of Brodie playing with his gun made him break out into a cold sweat.

But he wasn't willing to hide it, either. Not while Shayla and Brodie were in danger.

He slept fitfully, waking every couple of hours to walk around Hawk's cabin, peering through windows and making sure there was no one lurking outside. At two in the morning he thought he heard Brodie crying, but when he went over to listen at the door, he figured it must have been his imagination.

At six, he set about making a pot of coffee, craving a jolt of caffeine. He pulled out an old teakettle and filled it with water and set it on the stove to heat up. For some reason, Hawk didn't have a microwave.

Shayla emerged from the bedroom fifteen minutes later, her blond hair tousled from sleep. Her brown eyes were bright, though, giving him the impression that she'd slept well.

"I'd like to use your phone to call my dad."

"Sure." He unplugged it from the charger and handed it over. Sipping his coffee, he listened to her side of the conversation.

"Oh, he's already left for surgery?" Her face fell with stark disappointment. "Okay, thanks." She stared down at the phone for a moment before handing it back to him. "I just missed him."

"I'm sorry to hear that, but he'll be fine."

"I hope so." She crossed over, filled a mug with coffee and then joined him at the table. "I should have called earlier."

"You couldn't have known what time they'd take him." He desperately wanted to take her hand in his but wasn't sure she would be receptive to his touch. "We can pray for him again."

"I have." She was still avoiding his direct gaze. "I really want to go to the hospital to see him after surgery. I need to see him, Mike."

"We will." He hoped Hawk would show up sooner rather than later. "I had plans to head into town anyway. I'd like to stop by and visit Peter Fresno, your brother's partner. See if he has any idea where Duncan might be."

That made her look at him. "I'd like to go with you. I don't know Pete, but I'm sure he'd prefer talking to me as Duncan's sister than with a private investigator intent on sullying his partner's name."

His initial instinct was to refuse but he was forced to admit she had a point. At least about the part about Pete opening up to her more so than him. Visiting a cop hardly sounded dangerous, so he relented. "Okay, we'll give it a try. And I'm not going to smear your brother's name. I told you I'm willing to hear Duncan's side of the story."

"I know." She lifted her mug and took a sip. They sat in silence for a few minutes before she offered, "You asked about my pregnancy?"

"Yes." He leaned forward, trying not to appear too eager. "I hope it wasn't a difficult time for you."

"I loved being pregnant, but unfortunately I also suffered from gestational diabetes." She shrugged. "I had to watch what I ate, but even so, Brodie was a large baby. I ended up delivering him via C-section."

His stomach knotted with concern and a measure of guilt. His mother had complained about how big he was as a baby; was it his DNA that had created her pregnancy issues? "But you're all right now? No lingering problems?"

"I'm fine and so is Brodie." She stared into her mug for a moment. "My aunt Jean has been wonderful. I'm not sure what I would have done without her. She helps watch him while I work."

He knew that Shayla's dependence on her aunt was, in large part, his fault. For not listening to her when she reached out to him. For being obsessed with her brother and father's complicity in his father's murder. He should have been there for her, should have been paying child support.

Instead he'd missed his son being born, his first smile, his first steps... The list was endless.

He forced himself to remain focused on the present, rather than wallowing in the what-ifs. "What sort of work? Did you ever get into nursing school?"

"No. I'm a medical coder for a large hospital in Nashville, which is a fancy way of saying I read a lot of patient charts for billing reasons. It's not exciting by any means, but it pays the bills and offers me the chance to work at home, which is frankly more important as far as having flexibility with Brodie."

"That's nice."

She nodded but didn't add anything more.

"Mommy?" Brodie's voice from the bedroom had Shayla leaping to her feet.

"Right here, kiddo." She hurried into the guest room, then led him by the hand into the bathroom. He heard her praising him for being a good boy. They emerged a few minutes later.

How pathetic was it that he wished he'd had the opportunity to change his son's diapers?

"I'm hungry," Brodie announced.

"We have instant oatmeal for breakfast." He sent her a look, lifting a brow questioningly. "Hope that's okay."

"One good thing about having a kid who's always hungry, he isn't too picky. Instant oatmeal will be fine."

Brodie crawled up onto a kitchen chair. He was tall for his age, but didn't quite reach the table. Shayla brought in a pillow from the bedroom to give him a boost.

The teakettle whistled, making Brodie clap his hands over his ears. Mike made the oatmeal, adding a dash of brown sugar. Brodie gobbled it up and then asked for seconds.

"Told you," Shayla said wryly.

Hawk arrived ninety minutes later, bringing the phones and the computer and setting them on the kitchen table. To Mike's surprise, he handed Brodie a box of toddler building blocks to play with.

"Thanks," Shayla said with a smile.

The flash of jealousy was ridiculous and he wished he'd have thought of asking Hawk to buy something to keep Brodie entertained. Apparently he wasn't very good at being an instant father.

He quickly plugged in and activated the new phones, then opened the computer, intending to double-check the location of Fresno's address.

"Here are the keys to my SUV," Hawk said, dropping them onto the table beside Mike. "An army buddy of mine, Rock Miller, is waiting outside to take me home, so I have to run. Let me know if you need anything else, okay?"

"Will do." Mike stood and clapped Hawk on the shoulder. "Thanks."

"Oh, and I went back to the farmhouse last night and waited for your car to be towed. They arrived within an hour or so. I don't think anyone came back to look at your plates."

"Glad to hear it." Mike reminded himself that Hawk's assistance had been invaluable. "I appreciate everything you've done for me."

"Yeah, yeah." Hawk lifted a hand and left.

Brodie cried out with glee when his tower of building blocks toppled over on the floor. "Again, Mommy! Do it again."

Mike watched them for a moment, wondering how long he'd continue to feel like an outsider when it came to Shayla and Brodie. After verifying Fresno's address, he spent the next few minutes cleaning up the kitchen before heading into the living room.

"I'd like to leave soon, if that's okay with you."

Shayla glanced at her watch. "It's only nine thirty, a little early to go to the hospital."

"I know, but I'd like to stop by Fresno's place first and that's a good forty-five minutes away. We can head to the hospital after that. It won't hurt to get there early, and we can always get something in the cafeteria for lunch while we wait."

"Sounds good." Shayla opened the box and began putting the building blocks away.

"No! Wanna play!" Brodie thrust out his lower lip.

"You can play with them later, okay?"

"No, no, no!" Brodie swept out his chubby arm and sent the rest of the blocks sailing across the living room.

"Maybe he can have a few in the car," Mike offered, trying to find a compromise.

"Yes." Brodie nodded, eyeing Mike curiously. "I wanna play wif them in the car."

"Okay, pick two blocks." Shayla continued putting the rest away. "That's all. And you need to go to the bathroom before we leave."

It took another fifteen minutes before they were safely buckled in Hawk's SUV. Mike seemed to remember that taking his nieces and nephews on trips always took longer than expected and made a mental note to plan ahead next time.

The sun shone brightly in the sky as he headed to the interstate that would take them to the city of Brookland, where Fresno lived.

"Next time, don't override my decision," Shayla said in a low voice intended not to be overheard by Brodie. "It's not good for him to play one parent against the other."

He clenched his jaw but nodded. "Understood, although that certainly wasn't my intention. But that brings up something I've been meaning to ask you about. When can we tell him that I'm his father?"

She sucked in an audible breath. "I don't know. That isn't something I'm just going to spring on him, Mike. Maybe once this is over..." Her voice trailed off.

It was tempting to argue, to point out that it had already been three years and three months that he'd been denied access to his son.

How much longer was she planning to make him wait?

Shayla couldn't believe Mike wanted to just blurt the truth to Brodie without any thought of what impact it may have on the child.

Brodie wasn't going to understand why he didn't have a daddy before but had one now.

And the way Mike had butted in, offering Brodie the chance to bring two blocks into the car, annoyed her. He acted as if he had a right to interfere with how she raised Brodie, as if he were a childcare expert. She fully expected Brodie to lose the blocks, especially since he'd been smacking them together, enjoying the loud noise they made.

The oatmeal they'd eaten for breakfast sat like a lump in her stomach. As the miles passed, her anger slowly evaporated.

Maybe she wasn't being fair to Mike. She knew the

man she'd fallen in love with was a good guy. A man who'd come to her seeking solace the night he'd bitterly argued with his father. One who cared about others.

Everyone, except her family.

His father's death had changed him. She'd felt awful for what he'd been going through, but she also couldn't fathom the man he'd become. Angry, frustrated, obsessed and all too willing to believe the worst about her father and brother. She'd begged him to give them a chance, but he'd refused. Worse, he'd forced her to choose between her family and supporting him in seeking the truth about his father's murder.

A path that had brought them to this moment now, almost exactly four years later.

Brodie finally stopped the infernal banging of his blocks to say, "Mommy, I'm hungry."

She rolled her eyes and twisted in her seat to face him. "Brodie, it's not lunchtime yet. Why don't you sing some of your school songs?"

Brodie broke into a song that listed all the colors of a rainbow. She could tell by the broad grin on Mike's face that he enjoyed it.

"Do you know other songs?" Mike asked when Brodie finished.

"Old McDonald had a farm," Brodie sang. And soon Shayla and Mike joined in the chorus of *e-i-e-i-o*.

The song kept them occupied for the rest of the trip, and at ten forty-five Mike pulled into the driveway of a small ranch house owned by Peter Fresno.

"Why don't you stay here with Brodie for a few minutes?" Mike suggested. "I don't even know if he's home."

"Fine, but I still think he's more likely to open up to me," she said.

"I'll let him know you're here and offer him the chance to talk to you directly."

It wasn't a bad plan. She nodded and relaxed in the seat. "Okay."

She watched as Mike walked up to the front door. He stood for several moments when the door suddenly swung open. Her brother's partner was short and carried a few extra pounds around the middle. He stared at Mike and then his gaze swung over to her.

She pushed open her door and stepped out. "Pete? I'm Duncan's sister, Shayla."

"I've heard about you," Pete acknowledged. He stepped through the doorway and brushed past Mike to join her. "How's your dad doing? Duncan mentioned he's been sick."

Her pulse quickened at the mention of her brother. "He's having surgery right this minute."

Pete's eyes widened. "Wow, I had no idea."

"Have you talked to Duncan?" she pressed.

"No. I haven't spoken to Duncan in a couple of days. He asked for a week of vacation time and our lieutenant granted it without a problem, no doubt because your old man is our current chief of police."

She forced a smile, although she sensed his underlying animosity. Over the approval of last-minute vacation time? Or something more? "Can you be more specific about when you last spoke to my brother? I wouldn't ask if it wasn't important."

Fresno made a big show of wrinkling his brow and lightly stroking his chin. "I'd have to say it was the day before yesterday. I called to find out how his dad was doing and that's when he told me about the old man's upcoming surgery."

The way he kept referring to their father as the *old man*

grated on her nerves. "You're sure you didn't talk to him at all yesterday?"

A flash of anger flickered in Pete's eyes. "I'm sure. What's this about, anyway?"

"Why don't you tell us what you know about the Dark Knights?" Mike asked, coming over to join them.

The anger flashed again and this time she noticed Pete curled his fingers into fists. "I don't know anything about them, other than what I've heard on the news. Why? What do the Dark Knights have to do with Duncan going missing?"

Mike's eyebrows levered upward. "I didn't say Duncan went missing."

Pete narrowed his gaze. "That's exactly what you both insinuated. I'm not stupid, I'm a cop. I told you I haven't talked to Duncan since the day before yesterday, yet you keep pressing for more. It's pretty clear you're searching for Duncan and you decided to come here because I'm his partner."

The tension between the two men was palpable.

"Do you recognize the name Lane Walters?" Mike asked.

"No."

Shayla stepped up to play the role of peacemaker. "Pete, you're right, we are looking for Duncan. And as his partner, we thought he'd come to you if he was in trouble. Because he trusts you, right? You both have each other's backs, isn't that how cops treat their partners?"

"Absolutely," Pete agreed, relaxing his tense muscles. "I wish Duncan would have called me. I'm always willing to help him out of a jam."

"I'm sure you are," she said soothingly. "There's a chance Duncan may still reach out to you. If he does, would you mind giving us a call?"

"Here, you can use my number." Mike took out a business card and handed it to Pete. "Call anytime, day or night, okay?"

"Yeah, sure." Pete barely glanced at the business card or at Mike as he tucked the card deep into his pocket. "Hope you find him soon."

"Me, too." Shayla and Mike stood watching as Peter Fresno headed back inside. When they were alone again, she glanced at Mike. "That was odd."

"Yeah." Mike's expression was grim. "I don't think he'll be calling us anytime in the near future."

She bit her lip, silently agreeing with Mike's assessment. Pete might be her brother's partner, but she had the distinct impression that Pete didn't like her brother very much.

Or maybe he didn't like being partnered with the police chief's son.

Out of basic jealousy? Or because he was involved in something shady?

She hoped and prayed it wasn't the latter.

SIX

Mike was convinced Fresno knew more than he'd let on, but it was clear the guy wasn't going to confide in them. He drove Shayla and Brodie to Trinity Medical Center, his instincts screaming at him that something was off-kilter.

Neither one of them had mentioned Duncan was missing, yet that was the conclusion Fresno had instantly jumped to. Because he knew something? The disdain in the cop's tone when he'd spoken of the chief of police had betrayed an underlying animosity.

For Ian O'Hare himself? Or Duncan?

Likely both.

"Mommy, I'm hungry," Brodie said from the back seat.

He heard Shayla sigh. "I know, sweetie. We'll get lunch soon, okay?"

"Okay."

They arrived at the hospital at eleven fifteen in the morning. Mike parked in the structure adjacent to the building as close as he could to the entryway. Shayla held Brodie's hand as they walked inside and crossed to the elevator.

"I wanna press the button," Brodie announced.

"Can you find the number three?" Shayla asked. "You learned that at your pre-K program, right?"

"I'm three," Brodie said as he pushed the button for the third floor.

"Yes, you are," Shayla agreed.

Brodie held up three fingers at Mike, who nodded solemnly. He was impressed at how well his son knew his numbers. "You're a big boy, Brodie. Do you like your pre-K program?"

The child nodded, then shyly edged closer to his mother. Mike had hoped that his son would grow to be more comfortable around him but, so far, that hadn't exactly been the case.

Except for that brief moment when he'd told Brodie he could take a few blocks along for the car ride.

Would he be relegated to holding Brodie only while he was sleeping? The thought was depressing. He wanted, needed, to tell Brodie he was his father.

But Shayla wanted to wait. Was that a reasonable request? Or a stall tactic?

He had no way of knowing for sure.

The elevator dinged and Shayla once again took Brodie's hand as they exited. She went straight to the nurses' station and asked to speak to her father's nurse.

"Stephanie is taking care of a new admission, so it will take a few minutes."

Mike sensed Shayla's frustration and reached out to put a calming hand on her shoulder. "It's okay, I'm sure we'll hear something soon."

The five minutes passed with excruciating slowness. A frazzled redhead finally approached with a hesitant smile. "I'm Stephanie, did you need something?"

"Have you heard anything about how my father's surgery is going?" At Stephanie's blank look, she added, "Ian O'Hare?"

"Oh, I barely saw your father. They took him to the OR

just as I was coming on shift. Sorry." Stephanie shrugged. "And he'll likely go to the cardiac intensive care unit afterward, at least for twenty-four hours."

Beneath Mike's fingers, he could feel Shayla tense. "How will I know when he's out of surgery?"

"Go down to the family center on the first floor across from the chapel. The doctor will come to find you there." Stephanie hurried away.

"Why didn't they tell me that this morning?" Shayla asked, scowling in annoyance.

"We'll go there now, see if they know anything about your dad," Mike assured her.

They walked into the family center to find it jam-packed with people. There was a TV in the corner, a judge show blaring loudly. The moment they entered, he knew that Shayla and Brodie wouldn't want to stick around for long.

"My name is Shayla O'Hare," she said to the woman behind the desk. "I'm waiting to speak to the surgeon about my father, Ian O'Hare."

"O'Hare, O'Hare," the woman muttered, running her finger down a list of names. "Oh, yes, here it is. Looks like your dad is scheduled to be finished with surgery at eleven thirty."

Shayla's face lit up. "It's almost that time now. Will Dr. Torres come down here to talk to me?"

"I'm sure he will. Why don't you have a seat?" The phone at the woman's elbow rang shrilly. She turned away to answer it.

Mike glanced around but saw only one empty seat. He moved toward a spot near the wall, hoping something would open up soon.

"Miss O'Hare?"

"Yes?" Shayla immediately crossed over to the desk.

"Dr. Torres will be down soon."

"Thank you," Shayla said with relief.

An olive-skinned doctor wearing blue scrubs and a cap that covered most of his dark hair entered the waiting room a few minutes later.

He recognized Shayla and offered his hand in greeting. "Your father's surgery went very well. He's in the post-anesthesia recovery unit and will be there about an hour before moving to the cardiac ICU. You can see him there once the nurses get him settled."

"Thank you, Dr. Torres. I'm glad to hear everything went well."

"Your father is in remarkably good shape. I'll watch him in the ICU overnight, but if all goes well, he'll return to the third floor the following morning. Heart surgery patients typically stay in the hospital for three to four days."

"That's all?" Shayla's eyes widened in shock. "I thought he'd be in for a week, maybe longer."

"No, we've learned patients recover better at home."

"Okay, thanks again." Shayla turned back toward Mike after the doctor left. "We have an hour before we'll be able to see him, so we should probably have lunch."

"Yes, Mommy, I'm hungry."

Mike smiled, glad that Shayla had been given good news. "Let's get something to eat."

The cafeteria was just as noisy as the family center, but they were able to find an empty table in the back of the room. Brodie enjoyed his grilled cheese sandwich and fries.

"I wish Duncan was here," Shayla said with a sigh.

"I know." Mike briefly covered her hand with his.

"I didn't like his partner," she confided. "He seemed like a jerk."

Mike nodded in agreement. "I didn't get the sense that

your brother would call Fresno if he was in trouble. Do you know who he might turn to for help?"

"I wish I did." She toyed with a french fry, twirling it in ketchup.

"What about his friends from college?" Mike pressed.

She hesitated, then glanced up at him. "Ryker Tillman went through the criminal law program with Duncan and they joined the academy together."

Mike filed the name away, wishing he'd thought of bringing the laptop. "Easy enough to call him, see if Duncan reached out."

Shayla nodded, seeming happy to have another person to talk to. After an hour had passed, they headed up to the cardiac ICU, which was also conveniently on the third floor.

"Hello, my name is Lori and I'll be your father's nurse for the rest of the afternoon."

"Is he awake?" Shayla asked hesitantly.

Lori nodded. "He's still a bit groggy, but go ahead and talk to him."

Mike followed Shayla and Brodie as they entered her father's room. Ian O'Hare looked pale against the linens. The last time he'd seen Ian O'Hare, at his father's funeral, the guy had dark hair with just a touch of gray at the temples. Now all his hair was silver. Because of the stress of the job? Or leading a double life?

"Dad? It's me, Shayla. I'm here with Brodie."

Ian turned and opened his eyes at the sound of Shayla's voice. "Shay," he whispered.

"I spoke to the doctor. He said you're doing great." Shayla's voice was husky with emotion and Mike could see the sheen of tears in her eyes.

"Duncan?" Ian asked. "Did he find what he needed?"

"Duncan isn't here now, but I'm hoping he'll come by

soon." Shayla glanced at Mike, who shrugged. He had no idea what Ian had meant by his question. "What was Duncan looking for?"

Ian didn't answer right away, his brow furrowed as if he'd forgotten what he'd said.

"Dad?" Shayla leaned over the side rail so she could catch her father's gaze. "What is Duncan looking for?"

"Don't worry, Shay. He'll find it…" Ian's voice tapered off and his dark eyes closed.

Mike stared at the police chief thoughtfully. Was he rambling because of the medications he'd been given after surgery? Or was Duncan really searching for something?

And if so, what?

Or maybe the better question was who?

Shayla wiped the dampness from her eyes, not wanting Brodie to notice the evidence of her tears. She should be thrilled that her father was doing so well. The monitor overhead beeped in a soothingly steady beat.

After watching her father for a moment, shaken by how weak he looked lying in a hospital bed, she turned to Mike. "We can leave now, if you like. I don't want to tire him out."

Mike nodded. "We'll try to come back to visit later."

She smiled gratefully. "I'd like that." She leaned over the side of the bed and pressed a kiss to her father's cheek. "Love you, Dad."

He gave a brief nod without opening his eyes. As much as she wanted to stay, she knew keeping Brodie occupied for several hours at the hospital wouldn't be easy. Besides, she suspected her dad would sleep a good portion of the day and he needed to rest.

Where in the world was Duncan? And what had her father meant when he'd asked if Duncan had found what he was looking for? She knew Mike had noticed the com-

ment as well, and could tell his mind was already spinning with possibilities.

She led the way out of the ICU and into the hall. Brodie skipped beside her, seemingly unaware of how sick
his grandfather was.

"What did your dad mean about Duncan finding what
he was looking for?" Mike asked while they waited for
the elevator.

"How should I know?" She knew her voice sounded
testy and tried to maintain control. "It's probably nothing.
He just had surgery, I'm sure he had no idea what he was
saying."

The expression on Mike's face reflected his doubt but
he didn't press the issue.

"Uncle Duncan?" Brodie asked as they walked into
the parking structure.

Shayla looked down at her son in confusion. "Where?
Is he here? Do you see Uncle Duncan?"

"Over there." Brodie waved a chubby hand to their
right.

"Oh, no, sweetie. That's not Uncle Duncan." The man
standing near a parked car was decades older than her
brother.

She belatedly realized that her son was remembering
the incident from their first visit to the hospital when she
and Brodie and Duncan had stood hugging each other for
a long moment over the news of their dad's surgery. Then
a car had driven up and Duncan had abruptly pulled away
from her to go over to talk to the driver of the car. Her
footsteps slowed. She frowned, trying to remember. Had
the car been a black sports car, sitting low to the ground?
She didn't think so. Her brother had bent over to talk to
someone inside, but not as much as she imagined the
height of a sports car to be.

"Something wrong?" Mike asked.

"Huh? Oh, no. I'm fine." She forced a smile. "It's nothing. I just wish Duncan was here, that's all."

Mike nodded but looked at her with an odd expression, as if he were trying to read her mind.

"Do you mind stopping at a grocery store? I need to pick up another box of cheesy fish crackers."

"Not a problem," Mike readily agreed.

There was a store within a mile of the hospital and when they went inside, Brodie ran straight to the carts that were shaped like cars on the bottom with a wire basket on top. He eagerly crawled inside the car, making *vroom-vroom* noises as Mike pushed the cart up and down the aisles.

The errand didn't take long, although Shayla was overly conscious about how they must have looked like any other family out for a few groceries. In addition to the crackers she picked up a few essentials like milk, bread, peanut butter and jelly. They picked up a couple of frozen pizzas, too.

Mike pulled out his wallet.

"Oh, I can get it," she protested.

But he silenced her with a quick shake of his head. "It's the least I can do."

She held her tongue, understanding his need to do his part to support his son. It wasn't necessary. His determination to do what was right only reminded her of how much her life and Brodie's would change once the danger was over.

Once they were settled in the SUV, she quickly filled the plastic bag in her purse with fish crackers and tucked it away before Brodie could see them.

"We'll head back to Hawk's cabin," Mike said, pulling

out into traffic toward the freeway sign. "I'd like to find out where Ryker Tillman is located."

"Okay." She turned to look out the passenger's-side window, wishing she hadn't mentioned her brother's friend. She inwardly sighed and told herself to get over it. Finding Duncan was all that mattered right now. She feared her brother was in trouble, that his undercover work had somehow put him in grave danger.

As Mike drove, she noticed he kept glancing at his rearview mirror. The way he was constantly on alert should have been reassuring but wasn't.

It only reminded her of the danger they'd faced the day before. Meeting with Peter Fresno hadn't been enlightening, but it hadn't been dangerous, either.

"Mommy? I want my blocks."

She twisted in her seat to look on the floor. One of Brodie's blocks was down there, but from that angle she couldn't see the other. Stretching out her arm, she managed to pick up the blue block.

"Here's one of them." She lightly tossed the plastic block into her son's lap. "I don't see the other one."

"It's over there," Brodie said, pointing at the floor directly behind her.

Of course it was.

She had to unlatch her seat belt to get up on her knees, so she could see the red block. She managed to snag it with her fingers and handed it to Brodie.

"Don't drop them," she warned. "If you do, they'll stay on the floor until we reach the cabin."

"I won't." Brodie began to hit the blocks together in a way that made her wince.

Mike left the freeway, taking the highway leading to Hawk's cabin. But after just two miles, he hit the brake. "Well, that figures."

"What's wrong?"

"Construction. They're sending us on a detour." Mike turned left at the orange detour sign, the road barely wide enough to qualify as a highway.

"I hope we don't get lost." She looked around at the unfamiliar terrain. The flat farmer's fields had grown sparse as they'd headed into a wooded area.

"We won't. I have a good sense of direction." Mike's voice reeked of confidence and she found herself remembering how attracted she'd been to him four years ago.

Mike was the epitome of the strong, silent type. A rock under most circumstances, but he'd given her a glimpse of his underlying vulnerability the night he'd argued with his father.

The night he'd come to her, seeking solace, clinging to her as if he'd never let her go.

But he had let her go. Had pushed her away until she'd had no choice but to accept that what they'd once shared was nothing more than her imagination.

Pulling her thoughts away from the past, she noticed a sign announcing a narrow bridge ahead. She leaned forward, craning her neck to see the river flowing beneath.

"That's a big river," she said in awe.

Mike nodded. "The Wisconsin River runs from the northern part of the state all the way down to the Mississippi River. It's unusually high because of all the rain we've had the last two months."

Having been born in Nashville, only moving to Milwaukee when her dad had got a promotion within the Milwaukee police department, she didn't know very much about the state's history.

Mike slowed the vehicle as they approached the narrow bridge. It was a beautiful stone structure with two arches underneath and a thin wire fence lining the road on either side. The fence was disconcerting, not looking strong enough to stop a car from tumbling over the side directly into the rushing water beneath.

Lush greenery blanketed the shores of the river. Tall trees full of green leaves, no doubt getting sustenance from the fresh water.

They were almost to the halfway point of the river when a sharp report rang out.

"Someone's shooting at us!" Shayla instinctively ducked. "Mike!"

"Hang on," he said grimly. He abruptly hit the brake pedal and came to a screeching stop. Then he yanked the gearshift into Reverse and stomped the gas again, going back the way they'd come.

"What are you doing?" she asked.

"Trying to throw them off." Mike didn't let up on the accelerator, and Shayla instinctively prayed.

Dear Lord, help keep us safe!

Another gunshot echoed but there wasn't the sound of a metallic ping indicating they'd been hit. Had Mike's maneuver worked? The trees at the mouth of the bridge added cover, making it more difficult to see them clearly.

When they reached the end of the bridge, or rather the same place they'd originally started, Mike cranked the steering wheel, bringing the front end of the SUV around so that he could drive them out of there.

But he misjudged the angle, cutting it too much.

Shayla swallowed a scream as the back end of the SUV sank deep into the muddy shoreline. Mike shifted into gear and hit the gas.

The back tires spun, but the SUV didn't move.

They were stuck!

SEVEN

Panic gripped Mike around the throat. He hadn't been able to tell where the shooter was located and feared the gunman was already making his way toward them.

"We need to get out of here." He shoved open his door and scrambled out of the SUV. He hurried around to the other side of the vehicle, no easy task in the mud, to join Shayla. She'd pulled Brodie out of his car seat, holding his bag of cheesy crackers in one hand. The child's hiccuping sobs tore at Mike's heart.

"This way. Hurry!" he urged, indicating they should take cover beneath the stone bridge.

"I…can't," she protested, struggling to maneuver through the mud while carrying the added weight of her son. The mud was sucking at her feet, keeping her rooted to the spot.

"Brodie, I need to carry you for a while, okay? You're too heavy for your mom."

Shayla's stricken gaze caught his but she nodded and handed Brodie over. The little boy was frightened enough at the situation not to be concerned who was holding him. Brodie wrapped his arms around Mike's neck, holding on tightly.

Shayla stayed close as well, curling her fingers into the

back of his waistband. Without the added weight, she was able to pull her feet from the muck. He moved slowly but surely through the water until they were directly under the bridge. The sound of rushing water was louder there and he hoped the sound was enough to keep them from being overheard.

"It's okay. We're going to be fine." He spoke to Brodie and Shayla in a low voice, trying to keep them both calm. He was grateful for the shelter of the bridge and the towering trees overhead that offered some additional protection, too.

But their discarded SUV was like a beacon for the gunman. That and their muddy footprints along the shore.

"We can't stay here…" Shayla whispered as they huddled beneath the stone arch.

"I know." Mike reached into his pocket for his phone. He tried Hawk's number first but the call went to voice mail. Next he tried his brother Matt, who worked as a K-9 cop, and was relieved when Matt answered on the first ring.

"What's up, Mike?"

"We're in danger. I need you to pick us up ASAP," he said quickly. "We're hiding under a stone bridge roughly five miles off Highway 68 near the town of Cranton. We'll be on the north side of the bridge, across from where the SUV is located. Bring Duchess and a spare weapon because we'll be on the move."

"Will do." To his brother's credit, Matt didn't ask a lot of questions. "Keep your phone handy."

"Understood."

Mike's feet were growing numb from the cold river water and he knew Shayla must be feeling the same way. He wanted desperately to cross the river, but the water was deep enough that they'd have to swim. The May temperatures were mild but he knew being in the icy river could result in hypothermia.

Especially for Brodie.

But staying where the gunman could find them wasn't an option, either.

"We need to get away from the SUV," he told Shayla. "We can swim across and the water will carry us to that cluster of trees roughly twenty feet from the other side of the bridge. I know it's cold, but I don't think we can risk staying here."

"Okay. I can swim." What Shayla's tone lacked in confidence was countered by the steely glint of determination in her eyes. "Will you be able to manage with Brodie?"

"Yes. But he'll get wet."

"I know, but he'll be okay." She shivered and glanced up at him. "Ready when you are."

He nodded but then remembered his phone. "Wait. I need the bag of fish crackers for my phone."

Shayla nodded and handed it over. He carefully inserted his phone and zipped it shut. Then he put it in his breast pocket, hoping to minimize the risk of it getting wet.

Shifting Brodie in his arms so that the upper part of the child's body would be out of the water, he sent up a silent prayer for strength and waded into the river. Brodie cried because he was cold and gripped Mike even tighter.

"Shh," Mike cautioned. "We need to be quiet, okay?"

Brodie pressed his face into Mike's neck, muffling the sounds of his sobs. Mike knew it was the best they could do. When the bottom dropped away, he performed an awkward sidestroke, kicking with his feet to propel him across the river.

Shayla was beside him, doing her best to keep up. Ignoring Brodie's crying wasn't easy and he could tell it was bothering her. He wished he could have carried her across, too, but there wasn't enough time to make two trips.

They needed to get someplace safe and soon.

"I—I'm c-cold." Brodie was clutching him so tightly around the neck Mike found it difficult to breathe.

"Almost there," he said in a low whisper. "Remember, we need to stay quiet, okay?"

Brodie nodded but the sniffling sobs continued. Mike glanced around the river, scanning the shoreline for signs of activity. For several minutes they would be in full view of anyone nearby.

Was there enough time to get across without being seen?

He kicked again and again, fighting the current to stay on track to reach the cluster of trees.

His feet suddenly hit the bottom and he floundered for a moment until he could get his feet under him. Then he waded quickly up the riverbank to the base of the trees.

"We're safe now," he said, setting Brodie down on the ground. Glancing over his shoulder he noticed Shayla was struggling to get out of the water. He rushed over to help pull her to safety.

"Hold Brodie on your lap," he instructed. "And sit between these two trees. You need to share your body heat until Matt can get here."

"Wh-what a-b-bout y-you?" Shayla's teeth were chattering loudly.

"I'm going to take a look around." He glanced around, believing they were out of sight from anyone on the bridge, but still reached up to pull down a few branches, using them as cover for Shayla and Brodie.

"Don't go." Shayla reached out to grasp his leg. "Please stay with us."

"I won't go far," he promised.

Her fingers reluctantly dropped from his sodden jeans and he forced himself to move away.

After pulling his weapon out of its holster, he grimaced as water drained out. He'd learned while attending the police academy that a submerged gun may still fire, but without much accuracy. He shook the river water out and carried the weapon anyway. Accuracy may not be great, but he figured the gun might act as a deterrent. He crouched behind a clump of bushes, peering through the branches to see if the gunman was heading over to find them.

He listened intently, trying to pick out sounds different than the river. A movement along the shoreline on the other side of the bridge caught his eye and he narrowed his gaze when he realized someone was making their way through the trees toward the bridge.

Other than tightening his grip on his weapon, he didn't move. Tracking the gunman wasn't easy since he disappeared from time to time behind trees and brush. From this distance Mike couldn't even tell what the guy looked like.

Had the gunman seen them in the water? Maybe not, since it appeared the guy was heading toward their stuck SUV.

Unless there was more than one gunman. The thought made his blood run cold. Two gunmen would split up, each taking one side of the river.

Mike faded silently back into the brush, his heart pounding with adrenaline. He needed to get back to Shayla and Brodie. He'd protect them with his own life, if necessary.

Thankfully they were in the exact same spot tucked between the bases of two trees. With a frown, he realized they were shivering and instantly crossed over to kneel beside them.

"I caught sight of one man making his way to the SUV," he whispered, his mouth near Shayla's ear. "We need to stay very quiet in case there's more than one man looking for us."

Shayla nodded, although it was clear she was doing her best to keep her teeth from chattering.

"Let's sit together to stay warm, keeping Brodie between us."

She didn't argue, shifting her position so that Brodie was sandwiched between them. Mike wrapped his left arm around Shayla's shoulder, keeping the gun in his right, wishing he could do more. He hated knowing Shayla and Brodie were in danger. He knew they hadn't been followed and wondered if the construction ploy was nothing more than a carefully laid trap.

One that he'd driven right into.

He should have turned around and found a different place to stay. But it was too late for regrets. He needed to stay focused on their current situation.

Although he knew, only too well, that if anything happened to Shayla or their son, he'd never forgive himself. So he did the only thing he could.

He bowed his head and prayed.

Despite their soaked clothing, Shayla reveled in the warmth radiating from Mike's arm curled around her shoulders. And with Brodie warming up between them, she was relieved and thankful the boy had stopped shivering.

Sitting on the hard ground was far from comfortable, but she forced herself to ignore the rocks and twigs poking at her.

Mike's report of seeing the gunman moving toward their SUV was sobering. Especially if there was more than one of them out there. She couldn't hear anything above the rushing of the river and the thundering beat of her heart.

Why was this happening? Shayla could feel a surge of panic bubbling up inside and took several deep breaths in an attempt to ward it off.

Sensing her distress, Mike gently squeezed her shoulder and pressed a kiss to her temple in wordless support. She didn't want to consider the possibility that the three of them could die here.

Praying like the Callahans didn't come naturally to her, but that didn't stop her from trying. She wanted to believe that God cared about her and Brodie, despite their lack of formal religious teaching.

Please keep us safe, Lord. I'm sorry I never attended church, but I do believe in Your strength and grace. I hope You provide me a second chance to do better, raising Brodie to believe. Amen.

A low humming noise broke into her thoughts and she sucked in a harsh breath, glancing around in horror. Had they been found? Would the gunman silence them forever?

Her heart was beating so fast she felt weak and shaky. Then she saw Mike pull the plastic bag with fish crackers and his phone from his breast pocket.

"It works," he whispered in an awed yet hushed tone. He quickly pulled it from the bag and lifted it to his ear. "Matt? Where are you?"

Shayla couldn't hear the other side of the conversation, but just knowing Matt was calling brought a sense of relief. Help was on the way and she continued praying that Mike's brother would get there in time.

"Matt will be here in a few minutes." Mike opened

the bag to replace the phone when Brodie lifted his head, staring at the crackers.

"I'm hungry," he whispered.

If not for still being in mortal danger, Shayla may have laughed. Trust Brodie to be distracted from his fright by food.

Mike dropped several fish crackers into Brodie's hand, promising him more if he was a good boy and stayed quiet. As Brodie's mouth was full of food, the being silent part of the deal wasn't difficult.

"Stop! Police!" Matt's sharp tone, accompanied by a dog barking, made her jump. She glanced around but still couldn't see anything from their cocoon within the trees.

"Take Brodie," Mike whispered, pressing their son more fully into her lap. He took his phone out and handed her the bag of crackers. "I'll be back with Matt and his K-9 partner, Duchess, soon."

"Okay." Shayla hadn't known that his brother was a K-9 cop, but that explained the dog barking. She rocked Brodie back and forth, feeding him crackers until she heard the sound of footsteps.

She froze but relaxed when a large German shepherd came running over to them, sniffed the ground around them and then plopped down on its haunches, looking at her, tongue lolling to one side.

"Good girl," she whispered, trying to remember the animal's name. Queenie? No, Duchess. Having the dog was an added layer of protection and it was only another couple of minutes before Mike and his brother arrived.

"Doggy," Brodie said, reaching out to the German shepherd.

"She's not a pet," Mike quickly interjected.

"It's okay. Duchess is good with kids." Matt set a blanket down and knelt beside the K-9. "Friend, Duchess.

Friend." As he spoke, he put a hand on Shayla and then on Brodie.

Duchess leaned over to sniff at them, her tail wagging. Then she licked Brodie, making him giggle.

"It's all clear," Mike said.

Shayla gratefully stood, grunting with the effort. Mike took the blanket and wrapped it around her shoulders. "You okay?" he asked.

She nodded and leaned into him. "Thanks to you."

He drew her close, making sure not to squish Brodie, and planted a kiss on her temple. She found herself wishing he'd kiss her properly although, of course, he couldn't do that with Brodie between them. "Time to get out of here," he said in a low tone. "Unfortunately they got away."

"'They'?" she echoed. "Two of them?"

"I only saw one." Mike glanced at his brother. "What about you?"

"One perp, wearing black. And I only saw him from a distance. After I identified myself as a cop, the guy took off. I considered sending Duchess after him but worried he'd shoot her. Besides, it was more important to make sure you were safe. The minute I saw the cluster of trees, I headed over, figuring this is where you'd be hiding."

"Thanks, I appreciate you getting here so quickly." Mike clapped his brother on the shoulder and the look they exchanged, silent sibling communication and appreciation, made her wish Duncan was there.

"Let's get out of here," Mike said. "Matt, you'll need to lead the way to your car. I didn't see it anywhere."

"That's because I hid it and came in on foot." Matt's tone was smug. "Duchess does her best work on foot. Don't you, girl?"

Duchess wagged her tail again.

"Doggy." Brodie shifted in her arms, trying to reach down to pet the animal.

"Not now, Brodie." She shifted his weight in her arms in an effort to ease her sore muscles. "Later."

"Brodie? May I carry you for a while?" Mike asked.

Brodie immediately shifted toward Mike, raising his arms in wordless agreement.

The minute Brodie's weight was lifted from her arms, she wanted to snatch him back. Mike gazed at Brodie with a mixture of wonder and joy, making her eyes sting with tears.

Guilt washed over her, filling her with regret over the way she'd kept Brodie from his father. Oh, blaming Mike had been easy; after all, he'd pushed her away. He'd become obsessed with finding the person responsible for his father's death.

Accusing her father and brother of being involved in killing the chief of police had been the final straw. Even after that, she'd tried to call him.

But after that disastrous and one-sided conversation, she'd given up. She'd stayed in Nashville, rather than come home to force Mike to acknowledge the truth.

Worse, she'd convinced herself that she and Brodie were better off without Mike Callahan.

But she'd been wrong. So very, very wrong.

Tonight, she promised herself. Once they were warm and dry and safe, they'd tell Brodie the truth about Mike being his daddy.

Postponing the conversation wasn't fair to Brodie or to Mike. And the way he'd taken care of them, not just today but each time they were in danger, proved Mike would never do anything to harm them.

At least, not physically. Emotionally? She still couldn't say for sure. He'd agreed to listen to her brother's side of the story, yet she was convinced he believed Duncan was intricately involved in the Dark Knights.

She told herself she and Mike would work things out. They'd be fine, as long as she didn't give him her heart. Which meant no more dreaming about kissing him.

"Almost there," Matt said encouragingly. "I left my car behind those trees."

Catching a glimpse of Matt's SUV reminded her of the one they'd left behind. She turned to Mike. "We'll need Brodie's booster seat and may as well get the bag of groceries, too."

"Not a problem," Mike agreed. "Once you're all safe inside, I'll head back."

"I'll go," Matt offered. "I have a nonwaterlogged gun and a K-9 partner. Won't take but a minute."

"I thought you brought me a spare?" Mike asked.

"In the glove box." Matt tossed the keys in the air, grinning as Mike scrambled to catch them. "I'll be back soon."

"Crawl into the back seat," Mike told her. "We'll crank the heat until Matt returns."

She wasn't going to argue with that plan. Water still ran off their clothing in a seemingly endless stream, but she slid into the back seat anyway, then reached for Brodie.

"No. I wanna stay here."

She was surprised by Brodie's sudden attachment to Mike, although it made sense, after everything they'd been through.

"I'll start the car, then crawl in back with you," Mike offered.

She appreciated his gesture and scooted over to give him room. They huddled together, soaking up the warmth from the hot air blasting through the vents.

"I wish you were my daddy," Brodie said, leaning

against Mike. He let out a sigh, his eyelids fluttering closed as exhaustion claimed him.

"Me, too," Mike whispered. His gaze clashed with hers and the hint of moisture there was almost her undoing.

"You will be," she whispered back.

"Really?" His expression filled with hope. "How? We live in different states."

"I don't know, but we'll find a way to make it work." They had to.

Her son deserved a father. And he'd clearly chosen Mike to fill the role.

EIGHT

Brodie's words, *I wish you were my daddy*, echoed over and over in Mike's head. He was humbled by the boy's deepest desire and, for the first time since learning the truth, Mike was filled with hope and anticipation.

He was certain the look he and Shayla had exchanged was her way of agreeing to tell Brodie the truth. She'd said they'd find a way to work it out. Mike looked forward to telling Brodie he was his father and that they'd be a real family from now on.

Matt arrived with two bags of groceries dangling from one hand and the booster seat tucked under his gun arm. Duchess remained at his side, on alert.

Mike reluctantly shifted the sleeping boy into Shayla's arms so he could slide out of the SUV. He helped secure the car seat and then assisted Shayla in getting Brodie buckled in. The child woke up, rubbing his eyes with his fists.

"Doggy!" Brodie leaned forward, chafing at the buckle holding him back.

As if knowing what he wanted, Duchess jumped into the car, tail wagging as she licked at Brodie's face. He giggled and grabbed at her tail. Mike winced, but the K-9 didn't seem to mind.

"Come, Duchess," Matt called. Instantly the animal whirled around and jumped onto the ground to stand beside Matt.

"Is the doggy comin' with us?"

"For now," Shayla said, making no promises.

"I'll take these." Mike took the grocery bags and tucked them on the floor behind the front passenger seat. Shayla buckled herself in beside Brodie, leaving him to take the front with his brother.

Matt opened the back hatch of the SUV and Duchess gracefully jumped in. She pressed her nose against the wire mesh to sniff at Brodie. Mike closed the back and glanced at his brother.

"Shayla O'Hare and her son, Brodie, huh?" Matt murmured, lifting a quizzical brow. "Didn't you date her for a while a few years back?"

"Yeah." Mike shrugged and avoided his brother's keen gaze. "She's been living in Nashville but came home because her father is having open-heart surgery. She and her son are targets in this mess because of her brother, Duncan, or their father. Or both."

"Hmm." Thankfully, Matt didn't say anything more as they slid into the front seats.

Mike's brothers and sister were aware he'd dated Shayla, but he didn't think they knew how serious things had got between them. Which meant there was no reason on earth for Matt to suspect Brodie might be his son.

But even if his brother happened to traipse down that path of logic, this wasn't the time to explain the truth.

Mike found himself wanting to protect Shayla from the scrutiny of his family. What had happened between them was mostly his fault. He'd been the one to turn his back on his family and faith, seeking solace in her arms. He'd owned up to his mistake by proposing marriage.

Not because he'd had to but because he'd loved her. And thought she'd loved him.

But then his father had been murdered.

Her father and brother became his prime suspects.

Which had shattered their relationship beyond repair.

"Where to?" Matt asked once Mike started the car. "Hawk's cabin?"

He rubbed his hands over his face. "Yeah. We'll need to pick up dry clothes, though. Hawk may have some stuff at the cabin that I can use, but nothing for Shayla or Brodie."

"Good point." Matt looked thoughtful. "I should have thought to ask Lacy for some of her things, although nothing Rory has would fit Brodie."

"It's fine," Mike said. "New clothes are probably better anyway."

"I'll drop you off at Hawk's cabin first. You and Shayla can provide a list of what you need, including sizes." His brother looked at Shayla in the rearview mirror. "Is that okay with you?"

"That works," Shayla agreed. "But what about the SUV?"

"I called Noah," Matt said. "He and Mitch are going to pull it out of the muck and bring it to Hawk's cabin."

"Noah is Maddy's husband," Mike explained. "And Lacy is Matt's wife, and Rory is their one-year-old son."

"Wow, sounds like your family has grown since the last time I saw you. Lots of settling down." Shayla's smile was lopsided.

"Everyone except the Lone Wolf here," Matt said, lightly punching his brother in the shoulder. "He's been antirelationships for a long time."

Mike could feel his ears burning with embarrassment. Why did his siblings have to keep harping on his love life or lack thereof? His personal life wasn't any of their business. "Knock it off," he said gruffly. "Shayla doesn't understand your warped sense of humor."

"It's not warped," Matt protested.

"Lone Wolf," Shayla repeated from the back seat. "The nickname fits."

Mike swallowed a groan. "Just because I long for the occasional stretch of peace and quiet away from our rapidly expanding family doesn't make me a lone wolf. Now, can we please focus on something important? Like who the gunman is and why he wants to kill us?"

His brother's expression turned grim. "You have a good point, Mike. How did you end up near Cranton, Wisconsin, anyway?"

"The highway was blocked off with orange construction barrels and a detour sign was posted. Following the sign took us pretty far out of the way from the direction we were headed. I'm wondering now if the orange barrels were nothing but a trap."

"Could be," Matt agreed. "But that would mean the gunman would have had to figure out you'd be on the stretch of the highway in the first place. Which seems odd to me."

"I know." That part of the equation was bothering Mike, too. "The initial shots were aimed at Shayla and Brodie. They're the ones in danger."

"Start at the beginning," Matt suggested.

Mike reiterated the events that had taken place over the past two days. "I'm sure we didn't pick up a tail from the hospital because I kept a close eye on the cars around us."

"Could the gunmen have figured out you're helping Shayla?" Matt asked.

"Not sure how. The SUV we left in the muck belongs to Hawk. Although we were using my SUV last night. I guess it's possible the sports car took down my license plate number."

"Hmm." Matt looked thoughtful.

"Wait a minute." Mike pulled his cell phone from his shirt pocket. "If they did get my plate number, then it's possible they tracked my mobile phone."

Matt whistled under his breath. "It's not easy to trace a cell phone. Cop connections?"

Mike grimaced, unable to deny it. He lowered his window and tossed his phone out onto the side of the road. "I should have thought of it earlier. My carelessness almost got us killed."

"Hey, there's no way you could have known they'd track your phone," Matt protested. "Cut yourself a little slack."

Mike shook his head and stared at the landscape flashing past his window. He'd forced Shayla to get rid of her phone but hadn't done the same with his own.

Mistakes like that were unacceptable.

As much the nickname his brothers had tagged him with over the past few months annoyed him, he was forced to acknowledge that he'd earned it. After all, he'd decided to seek the truth about his father's murder on his own time, without telling them.

In a very lone-wolf type of way.

But now Shayla and Brodie needed his protection. Between his self-imposed duty to find the man responsible for killing Max Callahan and his desire to keep Shayla and Brodie safe from harm, he couldn't afford to be a lone wolf.

He needed his family's help.

The Dark Knights were responsible for his father's murder and also, he believed, for the danger Shayla and

Brodie were in. The two issues were interwoven in a complex pattern he still couldn't quite decipher.

But it occurred to him that after four years he was finally close to uncovering the truth. He only hoped that identifying the man who'd pulled the trigger wouldn't put the future he wanted to build with Shayla and Brodie at risk.

Shayla couldn't seem to get warm, despite the heat pouring in through the air vents. And if she was cold, it was likely Brodie was, too.

What if he got sick? His pediatrician was down in Nashville. A really nice guy, with kids of his own, by the name of Dr. David Pikna. She swallowed hard, battling a wave of panic.

It didn't make sense to worry about something that hadn't happened yet. Besides, she was fairly certain there were competent physicians in the area if she needed one. Maybe Dr. Pikna could refer her to someone here if needed.

She let out her breath in a soundless sigh. Never before had she been prone to panic attacks.

Then again, she'd never been shot at three times in less than two days, either.

And as far as she could tell, they were no closer to figuring out who might be responsible.

The way Mike had tossed out his cell phone had impressed her. She knew he was taking the attacks seriously. Then she inwardly groaned.

"Mike?"

He glanced over his shoulder at her. "What?"

"Your number was the one we gave the hospital. How will they get in touch with me if my dad's condition changes?"

"We'll give them the number of one of the disposable phones as soon as we get back to the cabin."

"I can pick up a couple more if needed," Matt offered.

"Sounds good. I guess I should have brought them along." Mike's expression was filled with self-reproach.

Shayla reached up to lightly touch his arm. "If you had done that, I'm sure they would have got wrecked by the river water. Everything worked out for the better."

"Not everything." Mike turned to stare out his window again. "But I'll do better going forward."

She caught Matt's gaze in the rearview mirror, seeing concern in his eyes. She lifted one shoulder in a helpless shrug, having no idea what to say or do to make Mike feel better.

One thing for sure, no way was Duncan behind any of this. Her brother loved her and Brodie. He'd never put her or his nephew in danger.

Deep down, Mike had to know that, too.

Twenty minutes later Matt pulled into the rutted driveway leading to Hawk's cabin. She unbuckled Brodie from the booster seat and lifted him out onto the ground. Matt opened the back of the SUV and Duchess bounded out, coming over to sniff at Brodie and then at Shayla, as well. Then she sat right in front of them, as if it was her job to protect them from harm.

"It must be amazing to work with a K-9 partner." Shayla rubbed Duchess between her tall ears.

"I'm fortunate to have Duchess," Matt agreed.

Mike lifted the two bags of groceries from the back seat and wordlessly carried them inside. She frowned, leaning down to take Brodie's hand.

"He's mad at himself, not at you," Matt offered. "Don't take it personally."

"I won't." She forced a smile.

"How old is your son?" Matt asked in a casual tone.

She hesitated, knowing if she told the truth he'd know that Mike was Brodie's father. "Excuse me," she said, leaning down to take Brodie's hand. "Brodie needs a hot bath and I'd like to get you that list. Have you ever shopped for kids clothing before?"

"For my son, yes. But he's only eighteen months old."

"Well, Brodie wears clothes in a 5T size. They go from twelve months, to eighteen months, like your son, and from there the sizes jump into toddler sizes, like 2T, 3T, et cetera."

"Five-T, huh?" She could practically see him doing the math in his head. "I think I can manage that." Matt unbuckled the booster seat from his vehicle and carried it inside.

She scribbled a quick list and then handed it to Matt. She felt guilty for deceiving him, but decided Brodie was Mike's secret to tell.

Mike had put the groceries away and come over to talk to Matt. "Before you leave, I need a favor."

"Another one?" Matt pretended to be put out. "Now what?"

"I have a box in my home office that I need you to bring here. You can stop for the clothes along the way."

"Yeah, why not?" Matt shrugged.

"Here's my key." Mike handed over a small house key. "Thanks, bro."

"Sure thing."

Shayla watched Matt drive away, wondering how long it would take before he returned.

Too long, and Brodie needed to get warm and dry now, not an hour or two from now. "Bath time, kiddo," she told him.

"Okay." Thankfully, Brodie didn't give her any trouble.

She scooped the sleeping bag off his twin bed and took him into the bathroom. Hawk didn't have any bubbles, so she'd used a dash of dish soap to create some. Brodie laughed and played, only putting up a fuss when it was time to wash his hair.

She dried him off with a towel and then wrapped him in the sleeping bag. Carrying him in the bulky bag wasn't easy, but she managed to get him into the living room near his building blocks.

While he played, she went back into the bathroom to wrap a dry towel around her shoulders in an effort to ward off a chill. Returning to the living room, she found one of the disposable cell phones Mike had charged the previous day and used it to call the hospital.

The nurse was nice enough to take down the new number. "I'll update your contact information in our system and write it down for your dad, okay?"

"That would be great," Shayla said with relief. "How's he doing?"

"He's resting at the moment, but his vital signs are stable. There's no sign of bleeding and his chest incisions look good. If he continues like this, I'm sure he'll go to a regular floor bed tomorrow."

"So soon?" Shayla couldn't hide her apprehension. It was inconceivable that her father could have his chest opened, his heart operated on and be out of the ICU in twenty-four hours. "There's no rush, is there?"

"No, but it's very typical that open-heart patients only stay a day in the ICU. It's better for them to be on a regular unit where they can get up and walk around. Don't worry, Dr. Torres is a great doctor. He'll do what's right for your dad."

"Okay, and that reminds me, make sure Dr. Torres gets my new number, as well."

"Not a problem."

"Oh, one more thing. Has my brother been in to see him?"

"I'm not sure. I haven't seen anyone, but my shift just started at three o'clock."

"Okay, it's not a big deal. I was just curious. Thanks again." Shayla ended the call, hoping her father's condition would continue to improve.

"No sign of Duncan?"

Mike's voice had her whirling around in surprise. She hadn't heard him come in behind her. She noticed he hadn't changed his clothes but held a pair of black jeans and a T-shirt in his hand.

"No. Duncan hasn't been in to visit, but the nurse says Dad is doing really well." She smiled, wondering why things seemed so awkward between them. "How about I throw in a frozen pizza for dinner?"

"Whatever you and Brodie would like is fine with me." He hesitated and then gestured to the bathroom. "I'm going to take a quick shower. Hopefully, Matt will return soon."

"I know." She tightened her grip on the towel she'd wrapped around her shoulders. "Brodie is warm, that's what counts. What's in the box you asked Matt to pick up?"

"Just notes and stuff." He didn't elaborate, turning away and disappearing into the bathroom.

Crossing over to the living room, she watched Brodie play. Being safe here at the cabin had helped her feel more in control of her emotions. Gazing down at her son, she thought the best time to tell Brodie the news would be right after dinner.

The next hour dragged by slowly. Her damp clothes were drying stiffly against her skin, driving her crazy. Finally she heard the sound of a car engine. "Is that Matt?"

"Finally, huh?" Mike looked relieved.

She took the bag of clothing from Matt and pulled out Brodie's things first. In addition to a pair of jeans and a rugby shirt with Spider-Man on the front, he'd included a pair of Spider-Man pajamas. "These look perfect, thanks."

"No problem." Matt smiled as Brodie picked up the Spider-Man shirt with excitement.

She took Brodie into the guest bedroom, so she could help him get dressed, then took out the plain jeans and sweatshirt she'd asked for. After sending Brodie out by Mike and Matt, she carried the items into the bathroom for her turn in the shower.

Being warm and dressed in dry clothes felt wonderful. She joined Mike, Matt and Brodie in the kitchen.

"Give those to me," Mike said, reaching for her wet clothes. "Hawk has a small washer and dryer in the bedroom."

The luxury surprised her but she nodded gratefully. "Thanks."

She looked curiously at the paper box sitting on top of the table. "Do you know what's inside?"

Matt shook his head. "Nope. But I'm heading out. Noah and Mitch will be here soon to drop off Hawk's vehicle."

"Okay." She hoped her relief that he was leaving wasn't too obvious. As she walked Matt do the door, she picked up the cell phone she'd used to call the hospital and tucked it into her pocket.

"Play wif me," Brodie said, coming into the living room. With a smile, she crouched down to play with Brodie. A few minutes later the phone vibrated in her hand. She quickly lifted the phone to her ear. "Hello?"

"Shay?" Her brother's voice sounded faint and weak.

"Duncan?" She jumped to her feet, glancing furtively over her shoulder to make sure Mike couldn't overhear.

Thankfully he was preoccupied with looking in the box Matt had brought from his home office.

Leaving Brodie with his blocks, she moved into the spare bedroom, closing the door behind her. "Where are you? Are you all right?"

"Are you still with Callahan?"

"Yes," she responded cautiously. "He's keeping me and Brodie safe."

"Good. Stay with him, understand? Don't go anywhere alone."

"I won't, but you're scaring me, Duncan. What's going on? Tell me where you are and we'll come get you. We'll stay safe, together."

"I can't. I just needed to hear your voice, but I have to go. Stay safe, you hear?" He abruptly ended the call.

As before, she tried to call him back, but he didn't answer. This time, his phone wouldn't accept messages.

The only good thing about the call was that she knew her brother was still alive.

But despite being shot at three times now, she knew her brother was in even greater danger.

Danger he seemed determined to face alone.

NINE

One by one, Mike pulled each item he'd collected out of the box, knowing it was time to come clean with his siblings. Four years ago, when he'd started investigating his father's murder, he'd realized that his family had all had the same idea.

But they had full-time jobs, too, just as he did.

His only advantage was that he worked for himself. Oh, he still needed to eat and pay his mortgage, but he could pick and choose what cases to take on. The flexibility of his private investigator role offered him opportunities his brothers and sister didn't have.

He wasn't proud of how he'd taken the information his siblings had uncovered without their knowledge, but reviewing everything together had been the best way for him to wrap his mind around all aspects of the case. Each of his siblings had identified specific details pertinent to the investigation.

Clues that he now had here at his fingertips.

He glanced over to make sure Brodie was okay in the living room, then sat down to begin reading.

The bedroom door opened abruptly. Shayla emerged, looking pale and shaken. She held one of the disposable phones in her hand and he quickly went over to her.

"What's wrong?"

She lifted her stricken gaze to his. "I heard from Duncan. He told me to stay with you, to not go anywhere alone."

"Duncan?" He tried to tamp down the incredulous tone in his voice. "He called you on the disposable phone? How is that possible?"

"I don't know," she said, shaking her head slowly. "But I know it was him. Who else knows I'm with you?"

He cupped her shoulders in his hands. "Shayla, this is important. No one has that number. So how did your brother use it to reach you?"

"I gave the number to the hospital," she offered. "I made sure the nurse had it and asked that she write it down for my dad, too. Maybe Duncan called in to check on our dad and got the number from them?"

"I guess that's possible." He felt relieved at the explanation but still didn't like it. What if someone else used the same tactic? The very idea made his blood run cold. "Tell me exactly what Duncan said."

She shook her head and set the phone on the kitchen table. "I already did! He didn't say much of anything, other than asking if I was okay and still with you. He told me to stay close and not go anywhere alone. I begged him to tell me where he was, so that we could come get him, but he refused and basically hung up on me."

The hurt in her voice made him wince. He gently pulled her into his arms, wishing he could say something to make her feel better.

To his surprise, Shayla wrapped her arms around his waist, burrowed her face into the hollow of his shoulder and hung on tight. He reveled in being able to hold her in his arms again, after four years of being apart.

She fitted perfectly, as if this was where she belonged.

He closed his eyes, wishing for a moment he could go back in time to do things differently. Having Shayla and Brodie here now was a second chance he was eternally grateful for. Yet he still grieved for everything that he'd missed.

Regrets were a useless waste of time, so he did his best to keep himself focused on the future.

Stroking his hand over her back, he rested his cheek against her hair. "I promise to do everything possible to keep you and Brodie safe, Shayla."

"I know." Her words were muffled against his chest.

He couldn't help himself from kissing her temple, the way he had earlier.

She lifted her head to look up at him. He lightly pushed the hair away from her forehead. "At least I know Duncan is still alive. That's more than we knew a few days ago."

He nodded, cupping her cheek in one hand. "I'm happy to know that, too. Don't worry, we'll find him."

"How?" she whispered. "We don't know anything about who's behind all of this."

It pained him to admit she was right. He knew the Dark Knights were involved but obtaining the proof he needed to convince his cop brothers to take action was proving impossible. He lightly stroked her silky-soft skin with his thumb. "I don't know, but I won't stop until I figure it out."

The corner of her mouth tipped in a lopsided smile. "I'm so glad to be here with you, Mike."

"Me, too." He searched her gaze for a moment then gently leaned down to capture her mouth with his. She tasted wonderful, exactly the way he remembered.

And when she kissed him back, his heart soared with hope and anticipation. Was it possible she still had feelings for him, the way he did for her?

The sound of wheels crunching on the gravel driveway

had him reluctantly raising his head. "Sorry, Shayla, my brothers have rotten timing," he whispered.

"It's fine." She looked flustered as she pulled out of his arms, smoothing her hair away from her face and taking a step back. "I have to check on Brodie anyway. And get the pizza in the oven. He'll no doubt be complaining that he's hungry soon."

Mike nodded, watching as she walked away to check on their son. He stood for a long moment wondering how she felt about their kiss. She hadn't pulled away, but she hadn't looked him directly in the eye afterward, either.

Did she regret kissing him? He sincerely hoped not. Shrugging off the hint of unease, he headed over to the door to greet his brother Mitch and brother-in-law, Noah Sinclair. Shayla disappeared with Brodie into the kitchen to cook the pizza.

"Thanks, guys," he said, taking the keys to Hawk's SUV. "I appreciate the help."

"Not a problem," Mitch assured him. "You helped bail me out of trouble when I was framed for murder, remember?"

"Yeah." He'd always been there for his siblings and it struck him how much easier it was for him to offer his help than to accept it. "I may need more assistance from you tomorrow. If you're up for it?"

Noah and Mitch exchanged surprised glances. "Absolutely. I can free myself up tomorrow," Mitch said. "I'm sure I can convince the others to come out, too."

"Agreed," Noah added. "Do you want to start tonight?"

It was a good idea. Mike hesitated and then shook his head. "No, I need to do a little research on my own first. Get my thoughts together. Tomorrow afternoon will be soon enough."

"Okay, sounds like a plan." Mitch grinned. "Two requests for help in one day, must be a new record."

Mike rolled his eyes at his brother's lame attempt at humor. "Whatever. Oh, and let me give you a different number for you to use to reach me." He crossed the living room to pick up the second disposable phone. Returning to where they stood, he rattled off the number. Noah and Mitch dutifully typed the information into their respective phones.

"I'll pass this along to the others," Mitch said, replacing his phone in his pocket.

"I'll make sure Maddy has it," Noah added.

"Thanks again." Mike knew he was fortunate to have such a supportive family. And as he watched Mitch and Noah drive away, he couldn't help but wonder if Shayla's family had once been the same way.

He knew what he'd overheard the day of his father's funeral. The words had echoed over and over in his mind. Was it possible there was a logical explanation?

Deep down, he prayed there was. He needed to understand what had happened to his father and why.

But even more so, he needed to find a way to keep Shayla and Brodie in his life. And uncovering the truth about her father and brother being involved in criminal activity would not help.

In fact, it could ruin his relationship with Shayla forever.

Disconcerted by Mike's kiss, Shayla put the pizza into the oven without preheating it. Mumbling "Idiot" under her breath, she pulled it out and turned the oven on.

She found comfort in the muted voices of Mitch, Noah and Mike coming from the living room. Knowing that the Callahan family was rallying around Mike provided a feeling of security.

They weren't in this alone.

Her brother and father would have done the exact same thing. If her father wasn't in the hospital recovering from open-heart surgery. And if her brother wasn't hiding from imminent danger.

Unfortunately, Mike didn't believe in her family the way he did his own.

"I'm hungry," Brodie announced, interrupting her thoughts.

"I know," she responded. "The pizza will be ready soon."

"Goody," Brodie said clapping his hands. Normally she didn't like giving him junk food, especially since he was already big for his age. She winced whenever the pediatrician weighed him. Dr. Pikna has assured her that Brodie was fine, despite being off the charts for both his height and his weight, but she still worried about him.

Yet, today wasn't the time to be concerned about junk food. Not after the way they'd barely escaped with their lives.

When the oven had preheated, she placed the pizza inside and set the timer. Mike returned to the kitchen and began packing everything back inside the box.

"Are Mitch and Noah gone?"

"Yep."

"You're not going to review that stuff tonight?" she asked, her brow wrinkling in confusion.

"Not until after we eat." After setting the box aside, he pulled out plates and cups and silverware, setting the table as if they were a family.

Which, technically, they were. She drew in a deep breath, reminding herself of her earlier promise. After dinner she and Mike would sit with Brodie to tell him the truth about Mike being his father.

Fifteen minutes later, the pizza was done. She pulled it out of the oven and sliced it. She cut Brodie's into smaller pieces, so that the sauce would cool and to encourage him not to eat too fast.

She carried the plates to the table while Mike filled their glasses with milk. Then he sat and held out a hand to her and to Brodie.

Confused, she placed her hand in his.

"Dear Lord," Mike said, bowing his head. "Thank You for providing this food we are about to eat. We also thank You for keeping us safe in Your care today when danger was near. We ask that You continue to bless us and to keep us safe from harm as we seek the truth. Amen."

"Amen," Shayla murmured. Mike's prayer touched her heart. She lifted her gaze and gently squeezed his hand. "That was nice, Mike. Thank you."

"You're welcome." His smile reminded her of happier times. The few short days they'd had together when they'd promised to marry each other, to care for each other and to love one another.

"Dig in, Brodie," Mike said, releasing his son's hand.

Brodie didn't hesitate. "Yum."

Shayla shook her head wryly. "He acts as if he hasn't eaten in days rather than hours."

"He has one voracious appetite," Mike agreed.

"We'll, um, talk after dinner, okay?"

He glanced at her curiously before recognition dawned in his green eyes as he understood the implication. "I'd like that."

She smiled and nodded, unable to shake an odd sense of uncertainty. Telling Brodie was the right thing to do, but even though she'd promised to find a way to make things work, she wasn't so sure there would be an easy answer.

Shared custody? The thought of giving Brodie up for weekends with his dad was unnerving. She told herself plenty of people did it all the time and survived, but the mere thought of spending so much time without her son had her curling her fingers into fists.

Would she have to move back to Milwaukee? Give up her life as she'd known it for the past four years in Nashville? And what about Aunt Jean? She depended on her aunt to help care for Brodie while she worked.

Her heart tripped and stumbled in her chest and she felt short of breath. Really? Another panic attack? What was wrong with her?

Stop it, she told herself sternly.

Mike frowned when he noticed she was picking at her pizza. "Something wrong?"

Wordlessly, she shook her head.

"More pizza?" Brodie asked hopefully.

She stood, took his plate and went over to cut up another slice. "Here you go."

"Thanks, Mommy." He ate another piece of pizza, grinning broadly. "My favorite."

"I think all food is your favorite," Mike said dryly. "Is there anything you don't like, Brodie?"

He scrunched up his nose. "'Shrooms and 'sparagus."

"Vegetables," Mike said with a smile. "Figures."

"But you like the little trees, don't you?" There was no reason to feel defensive of her son's eating preferences, but that was exactly how she sounded. "What about peas and green beans?"

Brodie nodded. "All good. Just not 'shrooms and 'sparagus."

"Well, then, next time we're at the store we'll have to

pick up some broccoli," Mike said with a smile. "Little trees are one of my favorites, too."

She rose from the table, carrying her half-finished plate to the counter. Nerves had stolen her appetite.

Mike and Brodie chatted while they finished eating, Mike asking questions about how Brodie liked preschool. She listened to her son's answers with a mixed sense of pride and dismay.

Being a single mother hadn't been easy, but Brodie was clearly a well-adjusted little boy. She hated the idea of tearing him from friends he'd made at the pre-K program.

"Are you all finished, Brodie?" Mike asked.

She steeled her resolve and turned to face her son and the man she'd once loved. "Let's sit in the living room for a while. I'll take care of the dishes later."

"I can help," Mike added, searching her gaze. He was so in tune to her emotions now, she found herself wondering why he hadn't been that way four years ago.

Maturity? Maybe.

She took a damp cloth and wiped the smears of tomato sauce from Brodie's hands and face. Mike went into the living room and lit a fire in the fireplace.

"Brodie, we have something exciting to tell you," she said. She sat on the sofa and brought Brodie up next to her. Mike took a seat on Brodie's other side.

"We're going to the park?" he asked, his brown eyes filled with hope. "I wanna go swimming!"

"Not right now, it's almost bedtime." She looked at Mike and then back down at Brodie. "Listen, Brodie, I want to tell you something important. Mike is your real daddy."

"My daddy?" Brodie glanced at Mike in confusion. "For today?"

"For always," Mike said. "I'm your daddy, Brodie. And I want you to know I love you very much."

"*4 for 4*" MINI-SURVEY

We are prepared to **REWARD** you with 4 FREE books and Free Gifts for completing our MINI SURVEY!

Romance

Suspense

You'll get up to...

4 FREE BOOKS & FREE GIFTS

FREE
Value Over
$20!

just for participating in our Mini Survey!

Get Up To 4 Free Books!

Dear Reader,

IT'S A FACT: if you answer 4 quick questions, we'll send you 4 FREE REWARDS from each series you try!

Try **Love Inspired® Romance Larger-Print** books featuring Christian characters facing modern-day challenges.

Try **Love Inspired® Suspense Larger-Print** novels featuring Christian characters facing challenges to their faith… and lives

Or **TRY BOTH!**

I'm not kidding you. As a leading publisher of women's fiction, we value your opinions… and your time. That's why we are prepared to reward you handsomely for completing our mini-survey. In fact, we have 4 Free Rewards for you, including 2 free books and 2 free gifts from each series you try!

Thank you for participating in our survey,

Pam Powers

www.ReaderService.com

To get your 4 FREE REWARDS:
Complete the survey below and return the insert today to receive up to 4 FREE BOOKS and FREE GIFTS guaranteed!

▼ DETACH AND MAIL CARD TODAY! ▼

"4 for 4" MINI-SURVEY

1 Is reading one of your favorite hobbies?

☐ YES ☐ NO

2 Do you prefer to read instead of watch TV?

☐ YES ☐ NO

3 Do you read newspapers and magazines?

☐ YES ☐ NO

4 Do you enjoy trying new book series with FREE BOOKS?

☐ YES ☐ NO

Please send me my Free Rewards, consisting of **2 Free Books from each series I select** and **Free Mystery Gifts**. I understand that I am under no obligation to buy anything, as explained on the back of this card.

❏ **Love Inspired® Romance Larger-Print** (122/322 IDL GNPV)
❏ **Love Inspired® Suspense Larger-Print** (107/307 IDL GNPV)
❏ **Try Both** (122/322/107/307 IDL GNP7)

FIRST NAME	LAST NAME

ADDRESS

APT.#	CITY

STATE/PROV.	ZIP/POSTAL CODE

Offer limited to one per household and not applicable to series that subscriber is currently receiving.
Your Privacy—The Reader Service is committed to protecting your privacy. Our Privacy Policy is available online at www.ReaderService.com or upon request from the Reader Service. We make a portion of our mailing list available to reputable third parties that offer products we believe may interest you. If you prefer that we not exchange your name with third parties, or if you wish to clarify or modify your communication preferences, please visit us at www.ReaderService.com/consumerschoice or write to us at Reader Service Preference Service, P.O. Box 9062, Buffalo, NY 14240-9062. Include your complete name and address.   LI/SLI-219-MSPC18

© 2018 HARLEQUIN ENTERPRISES LIMITED
® and ™ are trademarks owned and used by the trademark owner and/or its licensee. Printed in the U.S.A.

READER SERVICE—Here's how it works:

Accepting your 2 free books and 2 free gifts (gifts valued at approximately $10.00 retail) places you under no obligation to buy anything. You may keep the books and gifts and return the shipping statement marked "cancel." If you do not cancel, approximately one month later we'll send you 6 more books from each series you have chosen, and bill you at our low, subscribers-only discount price. Love Inspired® Romance Larger-Print books and Love Inspired® Suspense Larger-Print books consist of 6 books each month and cost just $5.74 each in the U.S. or $6.24 each in Canada. That is a savings of at least 18% off the cover price. It's quite a bargain! Shipping and handling is just 50¢ per book in the U.S. and 75¢ per book in Canada*. You may return any shipment at our expense and cancel at any time — or you may continue to receive monthly shipments at our low, subscribers-only discount price plus shipping and handling. *Terms and prices subject to change without notice. Prices do not include sales taxes which will be charged (if applicable) based on your state or country of residence. Canadian residents will be charged applicable taxes. Offer not valid in Quebec. Books received may not be as shown. All orders subject to approval. Credit or debit balances in a customer's account(s) may be offset by any other outstanding balance owed by or to the customer. Please allow 3 to 4 weeks for delivery. Offer available while quantities last.

▲ If offer card is missing write to: Reader Service, P.O. Box 1341, Buffalo, NY 14240-8531 or visit www.ReaderService.com ▲

BUSINESS REPLY MAIL
FIRST-CLASS MAIL   PERMIT NO. 717   BUFFALO, NY

POSTAGE WILL BE PAID BY ADDRESSEE

READER SERVICE
PO BOX 1341
BUFFALO NY 14240-8571

NO POSTAGE
NECESSARY
IF MAILED
IN THE
UNITED STATES

"I have a daddy!" Brodie kicked his feet with exuberance. "Just like Joey has a daddy."

"That's right. Just like Joey." Shayla smiled, glad her son seemed to grasp the concept.

"Are you gonna live wif us, forever?" Brodie asked, turning his wide, hopeful brown eyes on Mike.

"Yes," Mike said at the same time Shayla answered, "No."

"Joey's daddy lives with him," Brodie said, his gaze perplexed.

"But Carol's daddy doesn't," she swiftly pointed out. "Some daddies do but others don't. It won't matter, though, because you'll get to see your daddy all the time, right?"

Brodie seemed to consider that angle. "Right."

Mike frowned, pinning her with his gaze, but she ignored him.

"Maybe you and your daddy can play for a bit while I clean up the kitchen." She slowly rose to her feet, forcing herself to give Mike and Brodie some time alone.

"Can we play wif the blocks?" Brodie asked.

"Absolutely." Mike lifted Brodie down onto the floor next to the blocks, then sat cross-legged beside him.

Shayla hurried into the kitchen, wiping at the sting of tears. They'd cleared this hurdle, but there were many more to come.

As she scrubbed the pizza pan, she grew angry with Mike for rashly insinuating that he'd be living with them. That was something he'd had no right to promise Brodie. They hadn't even discussed co-parenting arrangements.

She took her frustration out on the pizza pan, washing with more elbow grease than what was required. Just as she finished with the dishes, she felt Mike come up behind her.

"We need to talk," he said in a low voice.

"You think?" She knew her tone sounded terse and drew in a slow, deep breath before facing him. "I can't believe you said that!"

"I was thinking we'd find a way to make it work. That's what you said earlier today."

"I didn't say we'd *live* together," she responded, keeping her voice down so Brodie wouldn't overhear. "I haven't agreed to move back to Wisconsin, either."

Mike hesitated and then shrugged. "Okay, I get that. It's reasonable that I be the one to relocate to Nashville."

Her mouth dropped open in surprise. "I—we—that's…" Her voice trailed off. She swallowed hard and tried again. "We shouldn't make big decisions right now. Not while everything is up in the air."

Mike searched her gaze, his expression serious. "Is this your way of telling me you don't have feelings for me?"

The question hit her in the stomach like a sucker punch to the gut. Because the problem was, she did still have feelings for him.

But love? No way. She'd already promised not to give Mike her heart. Not after the way he'd trampled it the first time she'd entrusted it to him.

"I don't know, Mike. Let me ask you a question. Do you still believe my father and brother have something to do with your father's murder?"

He opened his mouth as if to deny it and closed it again without saying anything.

"Yeah, that's what I thought." She tossed the dish towel on the counter and brushed past him, hoping he'd stop her. That he'd tell her how wrong he was for thinking the worst all these years.

But he didn't.

And that was an answer in and of itself.

TEN

Mentally kicking himself for not telling Shayla what she'd needed to hear, he listened as Shayla went into the living room to convince Brodie to put his blocks away. Their son made it clear he didn't want to get ready for bed, but she didn't take no for an answer.

He admired the way she stood her ground with Brodie. She was sweet, kind, gentle yet firm in her approach.

All in all, she was an amazing mother raising a well-adjusted three-year-old son. No thanks to any additional support from him.

"Say good-night, Brodie." Shayla's voice drew him from his thoughts.

His son came running over to him, proudly wearing his Spider-Man pajamas. "G'night."

Brodie hadn't said *daddy*, but Mike felt emotion well in his chest regardless. He scooped up the boy and hugged him close, pressing a kiss to the top of his head, breathing in the mingled scents of shampoo and toothpaste.

This. This right here was all he needed.

"Good night, Brodie." He didn't want to let the child go, but reluctantly set him on his feet.

"See you in the morning," Shayla said, avoiding his gaze.

"Yeah. Sleep well, Shayla." He wanted to go to her and

beg for a second chance, but she was already taking Brodie into the bedroom, closing the door firmly behind her.

He sat for a moment, staring blindly into space. Why hadn't he said the words she'd wanted to hear? He'd already told himself there could be a rational explanation for what he'd overheard the day of his father's funeral. No reason he couldn't have admitted that much.

Yet, deep down, he knew there was a connection between the O'Hares and the Dark Knights. He'd seen Duncan speaking with Lane Walters with his own eyes. And the meeting had been secretive, each man checking over their shoulders as if subtly aware they were being watched.

What did it all mean?

He scrubbed his hands over his face, battling despair. With steely determination, he picked up the box and began unpacking it again. If he examined all the pieces of the puzzle together, it was possible he'd find some sort of clue. Something they'd missed along the way.

Abruptly he straightened. What if he worked the case from another angle? Maybe from the assumption that Duncan and Ian O'Hare were innocent. A chill ran down his spine and he sat back in his seat for a moment, turning that idea over in his mind. For years now, he'd considered them guilty. Had that fact alone caused him to miss something important?

He couldn't deny the possibility.

Okay, then. He sat forward and began putting his notes in chronological order.

The Dark Knights had begun killing alleged criminals let out on the streets because the police and DA's office had failed to make the charges stick. Mostly because there wasn't enough evidence to prosecute or, in a rare case or two, where there was enough reasonable doubt that a jury had failed to convict.

The Dark Knights, proclaiming themselves a vigilante group of concerned citizens determined to make the city streets safe after dark, had killed their first criminal—a rapist known as Aaron Hine, who'd targeted college girls—six months before Mike's father's murder.

At the time of Hine's murder, though, the Dark Knights hadn't been a prime suspect and hadn't taken credit for Hine's murder. Mike had learned from various sources that Hine's murder investigation had centered on the fathers of the three female victims and the girls' respective boyfriends, but each one of them had had a solid alibi.

Hine's case had gone dormant for a month when a second seemingly unrelated incident took place. This one involved a murder of an armed robber who'd shot a convenience store worker, another young woman. The perp had worn a ski mask but had been arrested because of a video showing a tattoo on his arm and a store patron's recognition of his voice. Unfortunately the defense was able to prove others had the same tattoo, so he'd got off.

Mike spread out the two case notes. After the convenience store robbery, the clerk, who was a young woman named Lindsey Baker, had been left paralyzed. When the man who'd shot her ended up dead, the Dark Knights had claimed responsibility for the crime, pronouncing the streets were safer now for all young women. That had been five months before his father's murder.

There had been another murder each of the next three months, until the night his father had been killed while at the scene of an officer-involved shooting.

Why had his father become a target? Had his father had an inkling of who was behind the killings?

Mike pulled out a fresh piece of paper to take notes. Working under the assumption that his father had suspected cops were involved, Mike drew a line from his father to Ian O'Hare, who at the time was the deputy chief over internal affairs. If Ian was innocent, then he would have assigned several officers to investigate.

Who else had his father got involved? There had to be some sort of task force. Maybe one headed up by Ian? There would be other detectives added and, if he knew his dad, Max would have taken pains not to include any Callahan cops for fear of showing favoritism.

He shook his head, wondering how Miles and Matt had felt about that.

The heated words he'd exchanged with his father after graduating from the academy rang in his ears. His father could not comprehend why Mike had chosen to walk away from becoming a cop. Max Callahan had insisted their family's role was to serve the community and railed at Mike for being selfish, to have the gall to use the knowledge he'd acquired at the academy to start his own private investigation business.

Mike hadn't bothered to point out that his commanding officer, Sergeant Gaines, had held Mike in frank contempt, going so far as to claim Mike was riding his father's name and would be worthless as a cop.

Then there was the fact Mike liked detective work more than enforcing the law. Lastly, Mike didn't like taking orders. Not from Gaines or any of the other commanding officers.

He'd walked away, secure in the knowledge that he would be better off working for himself. Something his father had refused to accept or understand.

Dragging his attention back to the case, he began separating the evidence he'd collected over time. The bullet fragment from his father's body and the subsequent report related to the type of gun that was used were key in his mind.

He rose and walked over to make a fresh pot of coffee. This would be a long night.

Shayla didn't sleep well, and the blame rested on Mike's shoulders. Different scenarios flittered through her mind, Mike moving to Nashville, her returning to Milwaukee.

But most of all, it was how they would personally interact together in raising their son.

The kiss. It all came down to that toe-curling, heart-thumping kiss.

Pushing her tangled hair out of her eyes, she silently left her bed and headed into the bathroom. Brodie was still sleeping, a fact for which she was eternally grateful. Days like this, when she was exhausted from lack of sleep, it was better for her to have a cup of coffee under her belt before dealing with her son.

When she emerged from the bathroom a few minutes later, she crossed to the kitchen counter, surprised to find a half pot of coffee already brewed. She sniffed at the contents, confirming it was fresh, before pouring herself a cup. She added a dollop of milk before taking a sip.

The kitchen table was a mess, papers and items strewed over the surface. Did Mike always work in a messy chaos? The thought made her smile. Curious about where Mike was, she went into the living room to find him stretched out on the sofa, sound asleep.

Had he worked all night? The fresh coffee seemed to indicate he had.

She stared at him for a moment, his face relaxed in sleep, thinking about how handsome he looked. Mike's facial features reminded her of Brodie and she was a little shocked at how much their son took after his father.

As if sensing her gaze, Mike's eyelids fluttered open. He groaned and swung upright. "Good morning."

"Morning." She tipped her head, thinking he looked worse than she felt. "How long have you been asleep?"

He squinted at his watch. "About thirty minutes. But I also slept for a couple of hours between midnight and three thirty."

"Four hours isn't much."

"I've had less." He yawned and staggered to his feet. "I'll make eggs for breakfast after a quick shower."

Back in the kitchen, she took one look at the table and decided it was better to start making breakfast, leaving the cleanup for Mike. For all she knew, he had some sort of weird organization system going that she wasn't able to decipher.

Mike emerged from the bathroom, looking refreshed and cleanly shaved. He instantly began packing up his notes. "I thought we'd run to the hospital to visit your father today."

"You did?" She was pleased he'd thought of it. But then remembering the detour and resulting gunfire at the stone bridge, she frowned. "Are you sure it's safe?"

Mike hesitated and then nodded. "I have a plan on how to ensure your safety."

She eyed him warily. "What kind of plan?"

"My brothers are heading out here this afternoon and I thought we could get them to meet us at a designated spot where we can change vehicles. Kind of like leapfrog with cars. The next brother will meet with us at another location and we'll swap again. We can use the same technique on the way home."

"That seems like a lot of work," she protested. As much

as she wanted to see her father, periodic updates on the phone should work just as well, especially now that he was recovering from surgery. "I don't want to put your family out like that."

"They won't mind. Trust me, I'd be doing the same thing if the circumstances were reversed."

Was this some sort of backhanded apology for how things had ended between them last night? She appreciated the effort, but the idea of leaving the sanctuary of Hawk's cabin filled her with dread.

"I don't know," she hedged, turning back to whip the eggs. Brodie preferred them scrambled and she figured Mike wouldn't mind. "Let me think about it."

"Shayla." Mike's voice was low and husky. "I promise my brothers won't mind helping. A quick visit, then we'll gather back here to work on the investigation."

"You're still looking at the Dark Knights?" She shot a quick glance at him over her shoulder before turning back to pour the egg mixture into the frying pan.

"Absolutely." He sounded surprised by her comment. But before they could discuss the issue further, Brodie padded into the room, rubbing his eyes with his fists.

"Mommy, I'm hungry."

"Did you go to the bathroom?" Shayla asked. "The scrambled eggs will be finished soon."

"With cheese?" Brodie asked hopefully.

"Not today, kiddo." She hadn't thought of buying cheese. "Maybe next time."

"You heard your mother, you need to get into the bathroom." She was surprised Mike understood that three-year-olds who were recently potty trained had to be reminded to do such menial tasks. He took his son's hand and led him to the bathroom.

"Don't forget to brush your teeth," she called.

Mike waved, indicating he'd heard.

The toast and eggs were almost finished by the time Mike and Brodie emerged from the bathroom. Mike swiftly set the table and this time she was ready for his premeal prayer.

Mike's fingers wrapped warmly around hers. "Heavenly Father, we thank You for this food we are about to eat. We also seek Your strength and guidance as we follow Your chosen path while seeking the truth. Please keep us and our respective families safe in Your care. Amen."

"Amen," Shayla repeated, touched that Mike had included everyone in the prayer this time.

Even her family.

"Amen," Brodie said, picking up on their comment. "Now we dig in?"

"Right." Mike grinned, glancing at Shayla and reluctantly loosening his grasp on her hand.

She didn't like admitting that the one area she'd failed Brodie was raising him to attend church. That was never something her family had done on a regular basis.

Sharing Mike's faith was a bit humbling. And made her realize how faith and God were now an important part of his life.

But not enough of one to keep an open mind about her father and brother.

"Can I play outside today?" Brodie asked.

She glanced at Mike, raising a brow. "Do you believe it's safe?"

"I think so," he agreed. "We should have bought more toys to help keep him busy."

"Yes, well, running around outside will help him burn off some energy." She knew Brodie was getting bored with the building blocks. Normally she didn't allow Brodie a lot of television time, but even an hour of cartoons would have been nice. But since Hawk didn't have a television up here, that was a moot point.

"Sounds good." Mike glanced at the box of notes he'd set aside and she realized he wanted to get back to work.

"I'll take him outside," she offered.

He paused, shrugged and then nodded. "That would be great, thanks. And I'll clean up the kitchen."

She was about to protest but let it go. Mostly because Brodie was wriggling around in his seat, anxious to get outside.

When they were finished with the meal, she carried her dirty dishes and Brodie's to the sink. Then she took Brodie by the hand and led him into the bedroom to change out of his pajamas.

Before heading outside, she grabbed the disposable phone she'd been using, on the off chance Duncan would try contacting her again. Plus, she planned to call the hospital to check on her father, too.

If he was doing okay, maybe she'd talk Mike into skipping the visit. His leapfrogging with cars was a good idea, but also a lot of work.

"Play hide-and-seek with me," Brodie begged. "Me hide first."

"Okay, but don't go too far." Brodie's adventurous streak often got him into trouble. He seemed to have no fear of heights, and had been climbing things since he was a year old.

Had Mike been the same way as a boy?

"Ready or not, here I come," she called.

Brodie hadn't wandered too far away; she was glad to find him behind a clump of bushes. She chased him around for a bit, then agreed to hide so he could find her. They played until she was exhausted. Keeping a three-year-old busy was better exercise than an hour with a personal trainer.

She took Brodie inside for a glass of water and found Mike packing up his box of notes.

"Hey," he greeted her when she came inside. "Matt was able to free up his schedule early, so we're going to head out to meet with him. Noah will pick us up on the second leg of the journey."

"Are you sure about this? I called the hospital earlier today and Dad is doing great. I was able to talk to him for a bit. There's no reason to rush in to see him."

Mike glanced at her while continuing to pack up his things. "Actually, I'd like to talk to your dad for a few minutes. I believe he may have information that will help us."

"What?" Her joyous mood dissipated in a wisp of smoke. "You can't grill him about police work while he's recovering from open-heart surgery. Stress from his job is likely what put him in the hospital in the first place!"

"Shayla, I'm not going to grill him. I just need to ask if he has any suspects in mind who may be linked to the Dark Knights. A few simple questions, that's all."

Biting her lip, she turned away. She should have known Mike had an ulterior motive for creating the leapfrog technique of getting to the hospital. It wasn't for her sake at all.

It was for him. To find out once and for all if her father was at all involved in the murder of Max Callahan.

Well, he wasn't. Her father and brother would never condone taking the law into their own hands. And if it took a convoluted trip to the hospital to prove her point, then fine. They'd go.

But it was times like this that made her realize how much she and Mike had changed in the past four years. Every time he brought up her family, it widened the gulf between them.

Leaving Brodie as the only person who could bridge the gap.

A heavy responsibility for a child.

She gave Brodie a drink of water and then took him back outside.

Mike joined them a few minutes later, stashing his box of notes in the back seat of Hawk's SUV. She had no idea why he was carting everything along with them, and worried he planned to show some of it to her father.

"Come on, Brodie, time to go for a ride," she called.

Her son came running from the side of the house, carrying a stick in his hand like a sword. "Watch out, I'm gonna get you," he said.

What was it about boys and weapons? She opened her mouth to sternly tell him to put it down when Mike spoke up.

"Don't, Brodie. It's not nice to point sticks at people. You might hurt someone."

"You're not my daddy," Brodie said, sticking out his lower lip.

Shayla sighed, not in the mood for this. "Drop the stick and get into the car, Brodie. Now."

He looked as if he might argue, but she kept her I'm-not-kidding look on her face. He threw the stick down near her feet and climbed inside the SUV.

Mike looked crushed at Brodie's minor temper tantrum and, despite her earlier annoyance, she put a hand on his arm.

"Don't take it personally. This is why they call it the terrible threes."

"I know," he said, without looking convinced.

She slid into the passenger seat, while Mike got in behind the wheel. The SUV was facing forward, so it was easy for him to navigate Hawk's bumpy gravel driveway.

As they reached the road, a black sports car with tinted windows was coming toward them from the south.

"What in the world?" Mike gunned the engine, fishtailing it out of the driveway entrance and onto the highway. Except instead of turning away from the sports car, he headed directly toward it.

"Keep your head down," he shouted as he hit the gas pedal.

Shayla did as she was told, holding her breath and praying that Brodie would be safe in the back seat.

She thought she was prepared for the sound of gunfire but the sharp report followed by shattering glass was like a punch in her chest.

Please, Lord, keep Brodie safe in Your care!

ELEVEN

They'd been found at Hawk's cabin!

Sick to his stomach and ignoring the blood that ran down his face, Mike planted his foot on the gas pedal, putting distance between them and the black sports car. Wind rushed through his broken driver's-side window, through to the shattered passenger's-side window. It was distracting, making it hard to hear, especially accompanied by the sounds of Brodie's sobs, but forced himself to keep his attention focused on the road.

He figured he'd been cut by flying glass, but nothing more serious as far as he could tell. He was relieved that Shayla had ducked down in her seat in the nick of time to avoid being injured, although pieces of glass were scattered on and around her.

They had a head start thanks to his decision to turn in the direction of the oncoming sports car, but he knew that little number likely had more horsepower beneath the hood than Hawk's SUV. Thankfully, there wasn't a lot of traffic along the old country roads, although that was also something that worked against him.

There wasn't anyone nearby to report the gunfire to the authorities.

"Call 9-1-1," Mike told Shayla.

"I did" came the muffled reply. "They're sending a deputy to Highway 22."

He grimaced, realizing that at the rate he was going, they'd likely miss the deputy. "Call my brother Matt. I'll give you the number."

Shayla kept herself bent over in the passenger seat, but turned her head so she could type Matt's number onto the keypad. She put the call on speaker.

"Matt, the black sports car showed up at the cabin. We're headed south on Highway 22 and the sports car isn't far behind. I need you to meet us at the closest city where there are enough people to scare off the shooter."

"Got it. There should be another highway coming up, Highway 33. Head north toward Portage—that's a fairly big town. Plus the correctional institution is there, so there should be plenty of cops."

Mike was almost on top of the turn, so he hit the brake pedal hard and wrenched the wheel, managing to make a quick right without losing control of the SUV. Then he hit the gas again, hoping the sports car wouldn't notice he'd turned off the highway. There were enough tree-lined curves and hills to help hide the vehicle from view.

"I'll meet you there," Matt continued. "Head to the center of town and make sure you get into a public place. Let me know which one you choose."

"I will."

"Keep the line open," Matt added. "I want to know what's going on."

A glance at the rearview mirror confirmed the black sports car had kept pace. They were still about a couple of miles behind, but Mike feared they'd catch up before he made it to downtown Portage.

He'd never been there, but had certainly heard of the

correctional facility. He trusted Matt's instincts, so didn't hesitate. He continued speeding west as fast as he dared.

If there were as many cops in the area as Matt believed, he hoped one of them would pull them over.

The sports car steadily gained on them. Mike swallowed hard, silently praying for God to watch over them. He wished there was more that he could do to protect Brodie, who continued to cry from being scared. Thankfully the gunfire had been aimed at Mike.

Yet he knew Shayla had been the ultimate target.

He saw the sign announcing reduced speeds ahead. He hesitated, planning to ignore it, but houses and buildings were on the horizon and he knew he couldn't risk hurting anyone else.

"We're nearing the downtown section," he informed Matt. "You were right about the population."

"Find a place to go. A restaurant or something."

Mike slowed down enough to squint at the street signs. He turned onto Main Street and caught a glimpse of the Sunshine Café. There was a parking spot nearby, but he bypassed that in favor of a crowded gas station where there happened to be one spot left. The gas station wasn't far from the café. He pulled in front-forward in an effort to minimize the view of the SUV's broken windows.

"We'll be at the Sunshine Café," he told Matt before getting out of the SUV. "Hurry."

"Got it. See you soon."

"We're okay, Brodie," Mike said, trying to calm the child. He pushed open his door, shaking bits of glass from his hair and clothing as he ran around the SUV to Brodie's back seat. He quickly got the boy out of the car seat and handed him over to Shayla.

Brodie calmed down once he was in Shayla's care.

There was no sign of the black sports car as they

walked the short distance to the café. It was early for lunch, so the place wasn't as busy as he would have liked.

Easier to blend in with the crowds.

"A table for three?" a waitress asked, coming to greet them with plastic menus in her hand. She stopped and blanched when she saw Mike.

"You better go into the restroom to clean up your face, Mike," Shayla said in a low tone. "Yes, please," she said more loudly looking at the waitress. "Sorry about the mess, we happened to get in a minor car crash."

It wasn't a lie, the bullet had crashed into the car. And it certainly wasn't an accident. Mike clasped Shayla's elbow. "We'll all go to the restroom," he corrected, hoping she understood his need to keep them together.

"You're right. Please give us a few minutes, okay?" Shayla smiled at the waitress as they wove through the tables to the back corner of the dining room where the restrooms were located.

"Stay inside until I knock on the door," he said softly.

"Okay."

Mike waited until Shayla and Brodie were safely inside before ducking into the men's room. His reflection in the mirror made him wince. No wonder the waitress had looked so horrified. There was a lot more blood on his face than he'd realized.

Leaning over the sink, he peered at the cut on his temple. There was still a piece of glass stuck in there, so he used his penknife to lever it out. That caused more bleeding, and it took him a while to get it blotted off enough that he could wash his face.

Thankfully he wore black clothing, which helped hide the worst of the mess. Holding a wad of tissue to the wound, he left the restroom to check out where the back door might be located.

There was a hallway leading into the kitchen. He looked

through the window in the door, taking note of the location of the escape route. When the cook glared at him, he quickly turned away.

Satisfied, he lightly rapped on the women's restroom door. "Shay? You and Brodie can come out now."

Shayla emerged holding Brodie's hand. The boy's face had been scrubbed clean but his eyes were still puffy from his crying jag. He looked up at Mike with a frown. "You got an ouchie?"

"Yes, but don't worry, it doesn't hurt." He wished the stupid thing would stop bleeding.

"You look a little better," Shayla said unconvincingly. "We can ask the waitress for a bandage."

"That's fine." He glanced around the restaurant. The waitress had put the three menus at a four-top near the window. Unfortunately, that wasn't going to work for him. "We'll take this table in the back, near the restrooms."

Shayla didn't argue. Raising her voice to get the waitress's attention, she called, "Excuse me, miss? We'd like to sit back here, if that's okay with you."

The woman eyed them warily as she brought the menus over. She probably thought they were fugitives from the law, which wasn't too far from the truth. "Sure, no problem."

"Do you have a first-aid kit here?" Shayla asked. "We could use a few bandages, as well."

The woman reluctantly nodded. "I'll be right back."

Mike sat in the seat with his back against the wall so he could face the door. Through the wide window he could see traffic moving slowly up and down the main thoroughfare.

No sign of the black sports car. But he wasn't sure that meant much.

Had the gunman given up the chase? Scared off maybe by the corrections facility and the subsequent law enforcement authorities that were nearby? Or was he still out there, casing the joint? So far each attempt had been made when they'd been isolated from other people, but Mike wasn't sure that tactic would continue. The gunman could be feeling desperate, ready to take out innocent lives if needed.

Logically, he knew Matt was a good hour away, even pushing the speed limit. An hour that would likely feel like a lifetime.

The waitress returned with two bandages. Mike thanked her, as Shayla took them from her.

"Let me," she said, reaching up to remove the wad of tissue he had pressed against the cut.

He felt like an idiot, but couldn't deny appreciating the softness of her touch as she placed the two bandages over the cut in a crisscross pattern.

"Thanks," he said when she'd finished.

"Ouchie all better," Brodie announced.

"You're right, I'm much better." He smiled at Brodie, glad the child didn't seem too traumatized by the recent events. "I guess we should order something for lunch." He picked up a plastic menu.

"Chicken fingers?" Brodie asked. "And brown milk?"

"Sure." Shayla's smile was a bit watery and he knew at this point she wasn't about to deny their son anything. Even chocolate milk.

Their server brought over a coloring paper and three crayons. Brodie happily went to work on filling in the design.

"How did they find us at Hawk's cabin?" Shayla asked in a whisper. "Brodie and I were playing outside just before we left. If they had got there earlier..." Her lips tightened.

"I don't know," Mike said. "The only thing that happened out of the ordinary was Duncan's phone call to your disposable phone."

"Are you kidding me?" she asked in a harsh whisper. "You're blaming this on my brother? Will you give it up already?"

"I didn't mean—" he tried to explain, but she cut him off.

"Yes, you did. Face it, Mike. Since the moment we broke up, you've carried around a clear hatred for my father and brother. Well, I've had it. Don't you ever bring up Duncan's name in conjunction with anyone trying to hurt me and Brodie again. Do you hear me? Never."

He blew out a breath and nodded. He pulled out his cell phone and shut it down. She pursed her lips and then mimicked his actions.

He was relieved she'd done that much. He hadn't meant for it to come across as if Duncan had been the one to leak their location, but it was possible that since Duncan had got her disposable cell number from the hospital, the shooter may have, too.

Thinking about how close Shayla and Brodie had come to being shot and killed made him feel cold and nauseous. The only bright spot was that he'd brought the evidence with them from the cabin.

If it was still sitting on the floor of the back seat in the SUV by the time Matt arrived.

It was time to make a new plan. One in which he actually honored his promise to protect Shayla and Brodie.

Shayla was still trembling with fury when the waitress returned to take their order. She wasn't hungry but forced herself to order a chicken sandwich along with Brodie's chicken fingers and chocolate milk.

Mike ordered a burger. She'd turned off her phone because it was the smart thing to do, but she was still angry that he kept harping on her family.

"D'ya like my picture?" Brodie asked, holding it up for her to see.

"It's awesome," she said, leaning to kiss his cheek. The whole time Mike had been driving them away from the gunmen, she'd prayed. And thinking about those prayers now caused her anger to dissipate.

She looked up and caught Mike's troubled gaze resting on her. With a sigh, she realized fighting with him wasn't the answer.

"I'm sorry," he said, surprising her. "I don't believe Duncan would ever hurt you or Brodie. That wasn't what I meant to say. It came out wrong."

She slowly nodded. "Apology accepted. Although I'd be happier if you could look me in the eye and tell me my father and brother aren't involved in the Dark Knights."

His green gaze never left hers. "I believe they love you and would never hurt you. I'm not sure they're actively involved in the Dark Knights. I do think they may know something that can help us."

It wasn't exactly what she wanted to hear, but it was a start.

"I thought you may have looked at my notes on the kitchen table," Mike continued. "I'm working under the theory that your father, in his role of deputy chief over internal affairs, may have headed up a task force to look into police connections to the Dark Knights. And I think you could be right about Duncan working undercover to get information."

Her jaw dropped. "Really? Then why…?" She didn't finish because the waitress came over with Brodie's chocolate milk and two iced teas for her and Mike.

"You didn't let me explain," he said, picking up the thread of the conversation. "I thought the gunman may have pretended to be Duncan, calling in after a change in shifts to get your cell number. Not that Duncan gave it to anyone on purpose to find you."

She had to admit, that was the risk he'd pointed out to her. She reached across the table, holding her hand, palm upward. "Can we please agree not to argue about this again?"

He took her hand, his warm fingers closing reassuringly over hers. "Agreed."

"Me, too," Brodie chimed in, slapping his hand on top of Mike's.

She chuckled, staring for a moment at their three hands stacked one on top of the other. This togetherness was what she'd once longed for. Was that part of the reason she'd got so upset with Mike?

There were still so many unknowns about their future, but right here, right now, being with him felt right.

And protecting her heart seemed far less important.

When their food was brought to the table, she held Brodie back with one hand. "We have to pray before we eat, remember?"

Mike flashed a smile. "Yes, we do."

She took his hand and Brodie's as Mike did the same. It was a little embarrassing to pray in a restaurant, but she knew it was important.

"Dear Lord, thank You for this food we are about to eat and for once again keeping us safe in Your care. Amen."

"Amen." She looked at Brodie.

"Amen. Now we eat?"

"You may." Shayla cut his food into bite-size pieces.

Mike continued looking out the window over Brodie's head as they ate. She was grateful for his persistence. At one point, he shot to his feet but then sat again slowly.

Matt arrived about thirty minutes later.

Mike glanced at his watch, lifting his brow, and Matt shrugged.

"I got here as quickly as I could."

"Take my keys," Mike said, digging them out of his pocket. "My box of information is still in my SUV. You'll find it parked along the side of the gas station. The driver's-side window and passenger's-side windows are broken."

"Will do. I'll grab Brodie's car seat, as well."

"Thanks." Mike gestured for the bill after Matt left.

Shayla wished she had more cash on her, but she didn't. Mike paid, leaving a nice tip.

"Let me take Brodie to the bathroom one more time," she said as they left the table. "I'm not sure how long we'll be in the car."

Mike nodded and came over to stand like a sentry outside the restroom door.

When they were finished, Mike asked her to wait until Matt gave the signal. They quickly left the restaurant and piled into Matt's K-9 vehicle. Duchess wagged her tail in greeting.

"Nice doggy," Brodie said, pressing his fingers against the wire mesh.

"No other injuries?" Matt asked as Mike slid into the front seat.

"Thankfully not. But we need a new place to stay. Preferably family friendly."

"I figured. I have a place in mind, but it's a drive."

Mike glanced at her, then shrugged. "We can go to the hospital to see your dad later."

"I don't want to put him in danger," Shayla protested.

"Me, either," Mike agreed. "But sitting at the café for the last hour proves these guys are not going to risk being seen, or shooting at us with a lot of other people around. In that case, the hospital may be one of the safest places to be."

She had to admit he was probably right. Although a tiny part of her mind wondered how much of Mike's decision was influenced by his desire to talk to her father rather than concern for her feelings.

"Let's figure that out when we have you settled in a new place," Matt suggested.

The ride was long and Shayla was glad to see Brodie nodding off along the way. No doubt, a combination of having a full tummy and the effects of his crying jag.

When Matt pulled off onto a winding dirt road, she frowned. What happened to staying in a populated area?

Then she saw the dozen small cabins dotted around a large lodge. Several cabins were bigger and located near a playground, while others were smaller and tucked farther into the trees.

"This looks nice," she said with approval.

"Yeah, thanks, Matt," Mike agreed.

Matt slid out of the driver's seat and went around back to release Duchess. "I've already rented you a family-size cabin, so it will just take me a few minutes to sign off on the paperwork and pick up your keys."

Shayla climbed out of the car and stretched. For the first time in hours she felt safe. Their respective phones were off and no one other than Matt knew they were here.

She opened Brodie's door and gently nudged him. "Brodie? Time to wake up."

"Nooo," he whined, curling away from her. "Don't wanna."

It had been a long day and she figured he was entitled to be crabby. "Come on, don't you want to see the playground?"

That had him opening his eyes, looking around curiously. When she reached in to unbuckle him, he frowned. "No. I want my daddy!"

His demand stabbed her heart like a lance. Trying not to show her deep emotional turmoil, she wordlessly stepped back, granting Mike room to reach in to get their son.

TWELVE

Brodie had called him *daddy*!

Joy washed over Mike, making him smile as he reached into the back seat of the SUV to release Brodie from his car seat. It wasn't until he turned around to set Brodie on his feet that he noticed the wounded expression in Shayla's eyes.

"Wanna play on the swings," Brodie demanded.

"Ask your mother if she'll give you permission," he said in a firm tone.

Brodie looked up at her with large brown pleading eyes. "Can I, Mommy? Please?"

Shayla's stiff features relaxed in a tiny smile. One that didn't come close to reaching her eyes. "Of course."

Brodie latched onto Mike's hand, dragging him toward the swing set. Since Matt was still inside the main cabin getting their accommodations squared away, he lifted Brodie onto the swing and gave him a push.

His son's gleeful laughter was in direct opposition to the gunfire they'd so recently left behind. Mike felt a lump form in the back of his throat, the close call hitting him all over again.

Gut-wrenching to realize how close he'd come to losing Shayla and Brodie at Hawk's cabin. If he hadn't insisted on leaving at that moment to head back to the city to visit her father, the gunman may have found them.

When Matt and Duchess emerged from the main cabin, he stepped back from the swing set. "Come on, Brodie. Let's check out the cabin we'll be staying in for a couple of days."

His son ignored him, pumping his legs in an effort to leverage himself higher. "Push me again!"

He reached out and snagged the swing, bringing it to a stop. "You can play later."

"No! Swing now!" Brodie held on to the chains of the swing as if it were a life jacket and he were drowning at sea.

"Get down, Brodie." Shayla's stern voice was welcome. Having just become a father over the past few days, Mike had no idea how to handle a three-year-old's temper tantrum.

"Nooo…"

"Here's your key." Matt strode toward them with Duchess at his side. "You'll be staying in cabin number five, closest to the playground. Figured that would help with the little guy."

"Thanks." Mike took the key.

Brodie continued to wail in protest despite Duchess trying to gain the child's attention.

Mike noticed Shayla didn't show any outward sign of annoyance at their son's antics so he did his best to do the same.

"You want me to bring the box inside?" Matt asked.

"How do you feel about grocery shopping instead?" Mike asked, raising his voice so he could be heard above Brodie's cries. "I can give you a short list. We'll need something for dinner later and breakfast in the morning for sure. Plus some other basics."

"Why not?" Matt glanced at Brodie and grinned. "Wow. That kid has a healthy pair of lungs."

"Yeah." Mike rattled off what they needed. "Let me grab the box before you leave."

He followed Matt and Duchess to the SUV, glancing over at Shayla who stood staring up at the sky as if entranced by the clouds overhead. The intensity of Brodie's wailing had diminished some and he sensed she was waiting him out.

His admiration for her grew as he better understood that she'd been dealing with Brodie alone for the past three years. How on earth had she managed?

"I'll be back in an hour or so," Matt said. He opened the back for Duchess, then went around to the front to slide in behind the wheel.

"Okay." Mike shifted the box in his grasp so that he could free up one hand to unlock the door of cabin number five.

The interior was clean and quaint, not as rugged as Hawk's place as it was designed for tourists rather than as a man cave for hunting and fishing. He set the box on the table and poked his head into each of the two bedrooms separated by a full bathroom.

No doubt Shayla would approve. He thought about the wounded look in her eyes when Brodie had asked for him. Did she resent the idea of him getting close to his son? Having a relationship with him?

That didn't fit with the woman he'd known. The woman he'd fallen in love with. The four years they'd been apart had changed things between them and he was forced to acknowledge that their breakup was more his fault than hers.

But that didn't explain her reaction to Brodie calling him daddy. Unless that had somehow reinforced the fact that they had yet to make plans for the future. That they hadn't finalized any details for how they'd work things out once the danger was over.

"Ready to go inside now?" Shayla's voice wafted through the open door.

"Yeah." Brodie sniffed.

"Okay. Come on, then. We'll come back to the playground when you can be a good boy."

Shayla held the door for Brodie. The boy came inside, looking around curiously, his interest piqued by the new surroundings.

"Should we check out the bedrooms?" Shayla crossed over to peek at the arrangements. Just like at Hawk's cabin, one room had two twin beds and the other was the master. "This is our room, Brodie. You can pick which bed you'd like to sleep in."

He poked his head inside and looked around. "Okay."

Crisis averted, at least for the moment.

"I sent Matt out for food," he told Shayla. "I should have mentioned picking up a few toys for Brodie to play with."

"It's okay." She still hadn't looked him squarely in the eye. "The playground should help and there's a television here, too. Cartoons will keep him occupied for a while."

"Sounds like a plan." He hated the awkwardness between them.

While she took Brodie to the bathroom, he went back to pulling out evidence, determined to pore over every bit of it again with fresh eyes. There must be something he'd missed.

The first thing he pulled out was the article he'd kept for all these years, describing the scene the day his father was murdered. Mike was fairly certain he had every word of the article memorized, but reread it anyway.

> Milwaukee Police Chief Maxwell Callahan responded to the scene of an officer-involved shooting on Wednesday night, only to become a victim himself. As Chief Callahan approached the scene where Officer Rafe Scarletti had shot and killed an unarmed man, more gunfire rang out. Police Chief Max Callahan was hit twice in the back and pronounced dead at the scene of the crime.

The article went on to identify the initial victim as Curt Elliot, a young man who, while unarmed, was no stranger to crime. Elliot's rap sheet was longer than Mike's arm, his first arrest coming at the age of twelve and his life of crime ending with his fatal shooting at twenty-one.

Mike had gone to the crime scene about a week later. It wasn't far from a couple of two-story apartment buildings that he'd later learned were suspected to be owned by members of the Dark Knights.

There was no proof, though. The company that owned the property was listed as Rainbow Springs, LLC. But other than the name, he hadn't been able to find out anything else about them.

The cop, Rafe Scarletti, had been clean, too. Scarletti had claimed that Elliott had refused to pull his hands out of his pockets despite being told several times. Scarletti, having noticed something bulky in one of the pockets, and believing the perp had a gun, had fired his weapon when he'd noticed Elliot's hand moving inside the pocket.

Unfortunately the bulky items were several packs of cigarettes rubber-banded together and a bag of marijuana.

No gun. Not even a penknife.

Not for the first time, Mike wondered if Elliot had been shot on purpose because of his criminal record. It wasn't the type of shooting the Dark Knights were known for, but Mike felt certain they must be involved. His theory was that his father had been murdered that same day because he had made a point of going to the crime scene himself—something the police chief rarely did—and that the Dark Knights had panicked because they'd feared Max Callahan would uncover the truth.

Another name buried in the article caught his eye, causing him to frown. He'd forgotten that Elliot hadn't been alone that night. He'd been with a young man named Donte Parkerside, who'd been two years older.

Searching through his notes, Mike tried to find what information he'd uncovered about Parkerside. But there was nothing.

Had he missed the name completely?

Feeling the hum of anticipation, he quickly opened the laptop. Thankfully the cabin had decent Wi-Fi capabilities, probably one of the reasons Matt had chosen it. As a private investigator, Mike paid for access to a variety of search sites.

There were only two Donte Parkersides in the database he had access to, one much older than the other. Maybe a father and son? Mike decided to start with the younger Parkerside and instantly got results.

Parkerside had been out on parole after doing a brief stint in jail for armed robbery and aggravated assault. A shiver rippled over Mike's arms. Parkerside had injured a store clerk while attempting to rob her. The woman had been seriously injured but survived. As he stared at Parkerside's history, he was shocked the guy had got out of the slammer and out on parole because of "good behavior" after doing barely a year.

Normally aggravated assault and armed robbery was a five-year minimum. Mike noted that Parkerside had had a decent criminal lawyer rather than the usual public defender. The lawyer, Jake Stone, must have done some fancy footwork in front of the parole board to get Parkerside out of jail so early.

As he dug deeper, Mike uncovered the fact that Parkerside had only done a brief stint in jail after the officer-involved shooting. Parkerside hadn't had a weapon, either, but he'd been with a man who'd had drugs, which was enough to send him back behind bars for violating his parole. But not for long. Apparently a year later Donte Parkerside was, once again, out of jail and back on the street.

Mike began searching deeper into Parkerside's background, wondering if Donte could have been the original target. In his humble opinion, Parkerside's armed robbery and aggravated assault was worse than Curt Elliot's long history of petty crimes that included everything from theft, shoplifting, breaking and entering, and drug use.

Had the Dark Knights felt the same way?

He couldn't find any more arrests listed for Donte Parkerside and when another article caught his eye, he knew why.

Parkerside had been killed two and a half years ago in a drive-by shooting. A homicide case that remained unsolved.

Mike sat back in his seat, reeling from the knowledge that the two men who'd been there the night his father had been killed were both dead.

And the common link between them was the Dark Knights.

Shayla did a quick inventory of the cabin, keenly aware of Mike working on the computer at the kitchen table.

She'd told herself to get over Brodie's sudden attachment to Mike, but that wasn't as easy as it sounded.

This was the beginning of a new reality. From this point forward she and Mike would share custody of Brodie in some way.

Final arrangements to be determined.

Now that his temper tantrum was over, Brodie sat quietly in the living room watching a children's channel on the television. She'd wanted to smile at how uncomfortable Mike had looked during Brodie's meltdown, but managed to refrain. At least Mike had seemed to realize that being a father wasn't going to be all sunshine and roses. There were plenty of difficult issues to deal with, too.

But she had to give Mike some credit in following her lead. She'd expected Mike to break down, rushing over to offer Brodie something to make him stop crying.

But he hadn't. Instead he'd turned his back on the crying child, talking to Matt in a voice loud enough to be heard over Brodie's sobs.

Since Brodie was happy and quiet, she decided to enjoy the moment of peace by gazing out at the lovely wooded landscape, watching the few people who were staying at the other cabins. The place wasn't very busy. From what she could tell, only two of the other cabins were occupied.

She noticed Matt driving toward their cabin in the SUV. She crossed to the door and quickly walked outside to meet up with him.

"I hope I have everything you need," he said after stepping out of the vehicle. "I included a ten-pack of minicars for Brodie. Hope that's okay."

"That's perfect, thanks." She was touched by Matt's thoughtfulness. She held out a hand for a bag of groceries, but he waved her away.

"I have it. Do me a favor—let Duchess out of the back, then grab the door for me."

She did, following Matt and Duchess inside. Matt set the bags on the counter and began unpacking them.

"Thanks, bro," Mike said absently, his attention clearly on the computer screen in front of him.

"No problem. What are you working on?" Matt finished putting the few items away, then dropped down in a kitchen chair beside Mike. Duchess settled on the floor at his feet. "Who's Donte Parkerside?"

"He was another perp with Curt Elliot the night he was shot by an MPD officer," Mike replied.

She set the ten-pack of small plastic cars aside to join the men at the table, intrigued by their discussion.

"Parkerside was there the night Dad was murdered?" Matt asked.

"Yeah. He was also a known felon, had done time for armed robbery and aggravated assault, but got out early on good behavior. After the night Elliot was shot, Parkerside did another year behind bars, then was let out again. But within six months, he was killed in a drive-by shooting."

Matt whistled between his teeth. "That's interesting."

"I know. I can't believe I missed it my first time through all this." Mike sounded upset with himself.

"Hey, it's not your fault." Matt clapped Mike on the shoulder. "I've been looking into Dad's case in my spare time, too, but I didn't notice that there was another perp on the scene. I just assumed the guy who'd been shot was the key to whatever was going on."

Mike blew out a breath. "That's exactly the path I took. But knowing Parkerside was murdered after getting out of jail opens up more possibilities."

Shayla peered over to look at the picture of Donte Parkerside, but the guy didn't look familiar. She found herself wondering if her brother would have recognized him.

Thinking of Duncan reminded her about her father. It had been hours since she'd last spoken to him or to anyone on his health care team. "Mike, if you don't mind, I'd like to call the hospital, see how my dad is doing."

Mike instantly glanced up and nodded. "Matt, did you pick up new phones?"

"Yeah, but they'll need to be activated and charged." Mike's brother jumped up from the table and went over to pull the phones out of a big-box store bag. "I'll get going on these for you."

"Thanks," Mike said. "Shayla, is that okay? Can you wait a little while longer?"

"Sure." She wasn't about to argue. Not when she knew how close she and Brodie had come to being hurt or worse. Her gaze landed on the makeshift bandage she'd placed on the wound alongside Mike's temple.

Horrifying to realize how much worse it could have been.

"Mommy? I'm hungry."

Of course he was. She sighed and rose to her feet. "You can have a few crackers, but that's all. Dinner won't be ready for a while yet."

"Okay." Brodie's attention was diverted by a new cartoon that was starting. She put a small handful of fish crackers in a bowl and set it beside him.

In the kitchen, she pulled out the hamburgers and hot dogs Matt had picked up for dinner. She was about to pull out a frying pan, when she remembered there had been a small grill located outside the cabin. She headed out to investigate, hoping to find charcoal and starter fluid.

Everything she needed was right there, waiting for her. Once she had the grill going, she went back inside.

"Wait! I was going to make dinner," Mike said, rising.

"It's okay, I can do it. You and Matt are busy."

"Are you sure?" His gaze was a bit skeptical and she sensed he was still trying to make up for their earlier argument.

"I'm sure." She was about to add that she was used to being solely responsible for feeding Brodie, but held back. The tentative truce between them was better left alone.

Besides, deep down, she was relieved that Mike seemed to have dropped the idea of going to the hospital to visit her father. The last thing she wanted was for Mike to begin questioning her dad about the Dark Knights. Her father had already suffered a heart attack and open-heart surgery. He didn't need the added stress of being interrogated by Mike.

"We need the rest of the family here," Matt said abruptly. "By working together, I'm sure we'll find Dad's murderer."

"I don't know," Mike said, doubt lacing his tone. "Everyone is pretty busy with their respective careers and families. I know Marc and Kari's kids have just got over the flu. Miles and Paige just got back from vacation. And—"

"Hold up," Matt interrupted. "This is Dad's murder we're talking about here. Not one of us is too busy for that." Matt's gaze fell on the contents in the box. He frowned and stood up to see inside. "Wait a minute, is that my file folder of notes?"

"Uh…" Mike glanced away.

Shayla came over to see what the fuss was about. "What's wrong with the file folder?"

"There's nothing wrong with it, except that I had it at my place when it suddenly went missing. And these blueprints? Did you get them from Mitch?" Matt continued, digging through the items. He pulled out the evidence bag containing the slug taken out of their dad's body and he whistled again. "I can't believe it."

Mike held up his hand. "I can explain…"

"You took our stuff!" Matt looked dumbfounded. "Without telling us!"

"I was only trying to help," Mike said, trying again. But his brother wasn't listening.

"That does it. Since you helped yourself to our notes, we are absolutely going to work together from now on." Matt pulled out his phone and walked outside.

Mike dropped his head in his hands and let out a soft groan. "They'll hate me for this."

"No, they won't," she countered, coming over to sit beside him. "Oh, they'll be angry, but they'll get over it. Because families stick together no matter what."

Mike lifted his head to look at her. "You really think so?"

"I do. Just remember that same sentiment goes with my family, too."

Mike nodded slowly, reaching out to put his arm around her shoulders. "You're right. I'm sorry. I hope you can forgive me."

She rested her head on his shoulder, knowing she already had.

But that alone wasn't enough to fix everything that had been broken between them.

THIRTEEN

Mike savored Shayla's warmth, wishing there was a way to recapture the love they'd once shared. Those precious moments with her had been the best thing that had ever happened to him.

Followed shortly thereafter by his father's death, which had been the worst thing to happen to him.

"I need to call the hospital before I toss the hot dogs and hamburgers on the grill," she said, shifting away from him.

Reluctantly he let her go. His brother was still outside and Mike knew he deserved Matt's knee-jerk reaction about his missing file, knowing he should have come clean with his siblings a long time ago.

But he couldn't undo the past, either with his siblings or with Shayla, no matter how much he might want to.

Hopefully his family would forgive him. It was difficult to explain how devastated he'd been after their father died, a mere week after their heated argument. Illogical as it was, he'd felt personally responsible, as if somehow his decision not to continue being a cop had had a direct correlation to his father's murder.

His grim determination to find the man responsible for pulling the trigger that fateful day hadn't wavered over the years. Yet somehow, despite gathering all his siblings' information, he still hadn't been able to uncover the truth.

His gaze dropped again to the mug shot on the computer screen. Donte Parkerside was dead. There was no record or evidence of gang involvement in the drive-by shooting.

Struck by an idea, he searched for the young woman who'd been injured in Donte's aggravated assault charge. The incident had been an entire year earlier to the night of his father's murder. Lindsey Baker had been a young college student five years ago, a nineteen-year-old cashier, when Parkerside had decided to rob the convenience store the night she was working.

He could only imagine how frightened she'd been when he'd come in, demanding cash and waving his gun. She'd readily handed over everything she'd had, but Donte had still taken a wild shot at her before leaving.

Then the name clicked in his mind. But hadn't the Dark Knights already taken their brand of justice out on Lindsey Baker's assailant?

Unless there had been two perps that night.

Digging deeper, he discovered that Lindsey had been confined to a wheelchair since the event because the bullet had injured her spinal cord.

He listened as Shayla spoke to her father's nurse. From her side of the conversation, he could tell Ian O'Hare was doing much better. She finished the conversation by saying, "I'll talk to him later, then."

The idea of questioning the police chief about the Dark Knights lingered in the back of his mind. Shayla had reservations about him questioning her father, but he knew that they'd have to talk sooner rather than later.

If Ian and Duncan were working to find internal police

connections to the Dark Knights, then Mike wanted to know who exactly was on their suspect list.

"Hey." Matt's voice interrupted his thoughts. "Mitch, Marc, Miles, Maddy and Noah are all going to come up here tomorrow," Matt announced. "They agree this needs to be a team effort. From this point forward, your lone-wolf act won't be tolerated."

"Sounds good." Mike knew better than to argue. He met his brother's gaze. "I'm sorry. I didn't intend to make any of you angry."

"Yeah, we know," Matt admitted, although his brow remained furrowed. "But you should have come to us sooner. We could have been working together on this a long time ago."

Mike shrugged and held his tongue. That wasn't entirely true. Each of his siblings had demanding careers that had placed them or other innocent victims in harm's way. It wasn't even a year ago that Mitch had been framed for murder. And, honestly, the more time that had passed since his father's murder, the easier it had been to allow the case to take a back seat.

But not any longer. Witnessing Duncan O'Hare meeting with Lane Walters had jettisoned the case front and center. And now reviewing the evidence with fresh eyes, there were additional leads to follow. It wouldn't take long for the puzzle pieces to fall into place.

The only thing he couldn't quite figure out was why the meeting between Duncan and Lane Walters had placed Shayla and Brodie in danger. Every time they thought they were safe, the gunmen eventually showed up to finish the job they'd started.

Matt stared at him expectantly, so he nodded. "I'm sorry," Mike repeated. "I never intended to hurt you or the rest of the family."

"Yeah, yeah." Matt let out a heavy sigh. "It's fine. Do you need anything else before I leave?"

"Aren't you staying for dinner?" Shayla asked, entering the cabin. "You bought the food."

"No, thanks. Lacy and Rory are waiting for me at home." Matt's gaze softened when he spoke of his wife and son. "Lacy hasn't been feeling very well since the flu went through our house last week."

"Understood," Shayla said.

"We'll bring a replacement vehicle for you to use tomorrow morning." Matt headed for the door. "Maybe you could try really hard not to wreck it this time."

"I wasn't trying to wreck Hawk's car," Mike protested.

Matt chuckled and shook his head as he left the cabin.

Mike continued working until Shayla brought in a plate heaping with charcoal-browned hot dogs and burgers. Then he quickly put his notes away and set the table.

Brodie abandoned his television show to come running over to the table. "Hot dogs," he exclaimed, climbing up into a chair that Shayla had padded with folded towels to give him a boost. "Yummy."

Shayla turned the television off and then returned to the table.

Mike held his hand out to her, smiling when she readily took it. He reached for Brodie with his other hand and then bowed his head to say the blessing. "Dear Lord, we ask that You bless this food Shayla cooked for us. We thank You for keeping us safe today, and ask that You continue to guide us on Your chosen path. Amen."

"Please also keep my father and my brother safe in Your care," Shayla added. "Amen."

"Amen," Brodie echoed.

Mike felt guilty for omitting Shayla's family from his

prayers and realized she was right. Family always came first.

His and hers.

"Amen," he said before releasing their hands.

"Can I play on the swings after we eat?" Brodie asked.

Mike stayed silent, waiting for Shayla to respond. "We'll see," she said.

Brodie looked at Mike, playing one parent against the other. "You heard your mother," Mike said. "We'll see."

Brodie sighed but picked up a small piece of hot dog, dipped it in ketchup and popped it into his mouth.

"Maybe after your family arrives tomorrow, Brodie and I can go to the hospital to visit my dad," Shayla said.

Mike hesitated. "It's not safe enough for you and Brodie to go alone."

"I know, but there must be someone from your family who would be willing to take us."

"I'll do it," he said firmly. He loved and trusted his siblings with his life, but trusting Shayla and Brodie's safety with someone else? Nope, that wasn't happening. "I'll call Matt to put him off until lunchtime. That way we can head in early, before they converge on us."

She nodded and took a bite of her hamburger.

When they finished with dinner, he shooed her and Brodie outside. "You cooked, it's only fair that I wash the dishes."

"I don't mind," Shayla said, but he wasn't having it.

"My turn," he repeated.

"Come on, Mommy." Brodie tugged at her hand. "I wanna swing!"

Shayla followed Brodie outside, the screen door banging shut behind her.

Mike filled the sink with soapy water and then went over to watch them for a moment.

Brodie's laughter was contagious. The picture they made, mother and son, was so beautiful, his throat choked up. As much as he loved Brodie, Shayla was the one who captured his attention. He longed to run his fingers through her silky blond hair the way he used to.

Four years later and he'd never forgotten her. Had never replaced her with any other woman in his heart.

Gazing at her now, he knew he never would.

Shayla was the only woman for him. Unfortunately she didn't feel the same way.

And he was helpless to figure out how to make her fall in love with him again.

Glancing over her shoulder, Shayla caught Mike looking at them through the window with something akin to longing in his green eyes.

It had been sweet of him to insist on doing the dishes, giving her time with Brodie. Honestly, he was the one who should be out here with their son, making up for lost time.

When Brodie got tired of swinging, he ran over to the slide. He easily climbed up the ladder and let out a squeal of joy as he slid down the slick surface.

"That was fun," he said, running around to climb up the ladder again.

She thought it was good for him to be out in the fresh air getting exercise. Maybe he'd sleep better tonight as a result.

Brodie hit the ground hard, landing on his bottom during his fourth trip own the slide. He sat for a moment looking shocked and stunned, his eyes welling with tears. Before he could start howling, she hurried over to lift him up.

"You're okay," she assured him, brushing dirt and leaves off his clothing. "No bleeding. You'll be fine."

He sniffled and looked around as if to make sure she was right about the lack of blood. A stick caught his attention and he ran over to pick it up. "I have a sword!"

"Don't point that at anyone," she cautioned. "You'll get hurt."

Brodie made slashing motions with the stick/sword, hitting the tip against the ground. The stick broke in two and he looked again as if he might cry.

"Enough," she said, going over to take the remnants of the stick out of his hand. "Are you finished playing on the swing set? It's almost time for your bath."

"Swing," he demanded.

She pushed him several more times on the swing, until Mike came out to join them.

"My turn," he said. "Looks like you could use a break."

"Just a short one," she agreed. "Bath and bedtime are right around the corner."

Mike took over pushing Brodie, getting the child higher in the air than she'd been able to. Glad for a few minutes alone, she went back inside the cabin and picked up one of the disposable phones. Earlier she hadn't been able to talk directly to her father because he'd been off the floor for a chest X-ray. She dialed the number directly to his room, hoping he was back and able to talk.

"Hello?" Her father's low, husky voice answered on the third ring.

"Dad? It's Shayla. How are you feeling?"

"Pretty good," he said. "I was up for a walk earlier, made it all the way down the hall and back without any trouble."

"That's amazing." Just two days ago he'd had major surgery and now he was up walking around. "Your nurse tells me you're doing great."

"Dr. Torres says I can go home on Saturday or Sunday."

Today was Friday. "So soon!"

"Yep. I can't go back to work for several weeks, but they prefer patients recuperate at home."

Normally she'd be all for that approach but not now. Not when her brother was in hiding and she was being hunted by some crazy gunman. What if her father was also in danger?

She told herself that the Dark Knights wouldn't dare murder another chief of police just four years after the previous chief had been killed. But desperate people did desperate things.

"Well…" She cleared her throat. "I'm sure Dr. Torres will make sure you're stable enough to be discharged."

"Yeah." Her father was silent for a moment before he asked, "Shayla, where has Duncan been?"

She froze, her mind racing with how much she should tell him. "He's been really busy."

"I haven't seen him since before I went for surgery."

"I know." She was a little surprised that her father had been cognizant enough to figure it out. The few times she'd visited, he'd seemed a little confused.

"Is something wrong?" His blunt question caught her off guard.

"I'm not sure," she hedged. "I've spoken to him over the phone a few times since your surgery. I've been keeping him updated on how well you're doing. He sends his love."

Her father sighed. "It's my fault," he said in a low voice. "I'm afraid he's in danger."

The last thing she wanted to admit was that she and Brodie were in danger, too. "I'm sure he's fine, Dad. I spoke to Duncan yesterday."

"Not today?" her father persisted.

Dread seeped into her heart. "No, not today. Why? What's going on?"

Her father was silent for so long, she feared he'd hung up or fallen asleep.

"Dad?" she prompted.

"I need to talk to Duncan," he finally said. "If he calls you, will you let him know?"

"Yes, but what's going on? Is there something I can do?" She didn't like his ominous tone.

"Stay safe," her father said. "No need to come visit. I'm fine. Maybe you should head home to Nashville. I'm sure Aunt Jean misses Brodie."

She tightened her grip on the phone. "Dad, please, tell me what's going on! Why is Duncan in danger?"

"Goodbye, Shayla." Her dad disconnected from the line, much the way Duncan had the last couple of times she'd spoken to him.

Fear gnawed its way under her skin.

She knew now that Duncan must be working undercover with the Dark Knights at her father's direction. Hearing the concern in her father's voice was troubling. As the chief of police, he normally held his emotions under strict control.

Her dad worrying about Duncan couldn't be good.

Brodie and Mike came in, so she pushed her fear aside and pasted a smile on her face. "Bath time."

Brodie liked taking a bath so he nodded and dashed into their room. She went into the bathroom to fill the tub.

Mike went back to his notes while she bathed Brodie, washing away the day's dust and dirt that her son attracted like a magnet.

She felt Mike's gaze and turned to see him lingering in the doorway. "Has he always loved taking baths?"

"Yes. Any excuse to splash and play. He's been taking swimming lessons for the last year, too."

He nodded. "Smart."

Mike lingered as she finished with Brodie, drying him off and putting on a new pair of Spider-Man pajamas courtesy of Matt's earlier trip to the store.

"Tell me a story," Brodie begged when she tucked him into the twin bed he'd chosen.

She had several of his books memorized, so she settled in beside him and began to tell him the story about a bunny sleeping in a great green room.

"'Good night, room. Good night, moon,'" Shayla said in a soft rhythmical tone.

Brodie smiled at the familiar words to his favorite book.

She continued to tell the story until Brodie's long eyelashes drifted shut. Even then she didn't stop until she reached the last two words. "The end."

Brodie didn't move, his sturdy frame lax with sleep. She pressed a kiss to the top of his head before slipping out of the room.

Mike glanced up at her when she entered the kitchen. "Everything okay?"

She knew he was talking about Brodie, but her earlier fears about her father and brother resurfaced. "Sure."

Her voice must not have been convincing.

"What's wrong?"

She shook her head, rubbing her hands up and down her arms. "It's nothing. I'm going to take a little walk." Without waiting for a response, she left the cabin.

Dusk had fallen and a gentle breeze rippled through the leaves on the trees. She drew in a deep breath, trying to wrestle her emotions under control.

Unable to relax, she headed toward a well-worn hiking path. She hadn't gone very far when Mike called her name.

"Shayla? Wait up!"

There was a part of her that wanted to keep going, but then she realized Brodie was back in the cabin, so she turned around and met up with Mike.

"We can't leave Brodie alone," she said, brushing past him to head back to the cabin. It was only a few yards, but still.

"Shayla, what is it? What's wrong?"

He caught up with her at the front door, his hand capturing hers. She stared at their joined hands for a moment before relenting. "I spoke to my dad earlier. I think... Well...he basically told me Duncan is in danger."

Mike was silent for a long moment and she was sure he was wishing that they'd gone to the hospital together to question her father about the Dark Knights. "Did he say anything else?"

"Not really. That was the thing that bothered me the most." She swallowed hard. "He mentioned that Duncan was in trouble and told me to go back to Nashville. When I pressed him for more information, he told me goodbye. Not good-night, like he'd see me soon, but goodbye."

Mike's fingers gently tightened around hers. "I'm sorry. It sounds like he's trying to protect you."

Her eyes welled with tears and she blinked in an effort to ward them off. "I know. I believe my dad asked Duncan to do undercover work to expose the Dark Knights, but I'm worried that my brother is out there alone, without any additional support. And if his cover is blown..." She couldn't finish.

"It will be okay." Mike pulled her close and she leaned gratefully against him. His strong arms held her close and she sent up a prayer of thanks that God had sent Mike to protect her and their son.

"Shayla." The way he said her name in a hoarse whisper sent a shiver of awareness down her spine.

She lifted her head, looking up at him in the dim light. The way he gazed down at her, his expression full of admiration, made her heart squeeze in her chest.

"Michael," she whispered back. His family had always used his nickname but when things had grown serious between them, she'd used his full name.

He smiled at the memory. Unable to stop herself, she lifted up on her tippy toes and pressed her mouth against his.

This time the kiss was long and unhurried, his mouth thoroughly exploring hers. She clung to his shoulders, the world spinning crazily around them.

The last four years drifted away, taking the anger, the resentment and the regrets with it.

Leaving room for hope and love to be nurtured and grown.

FOURTEEN

He loved cradling Shayla in his arms. He absolutely didn't want their kiss to end. But eventually they needed to breathe. When he lifted his head to gulp oxygen, he tucked her head beneath his chin.

"You scared me when you headed into the woods like that," he said.

"I'm sorry. It was all just too much. Especially when my dad told me to head back to Nashville to stay with Aunt Jean."

His arms reflexively tightened. "You're not leaving," he said, trying to make it a question rather than a demand.

"No, I'm not. I can't bring danger to Aunt Jean's doorstep. Besides, I feel safe with you."

"I'm glad," he whispered. He wanted to know what else her father had said but knew he needed to tread lightly. She hadn't liked the idea of him questioning her father about the Dark Knights. "You spoke to Duncan yesterday, right?"

"Yes. And I told my dad that, too. But he didn't seem consoled by that fact."

His pulse kicked up a notch. "Did he say anything else about Duncan?"

"No." She lifted her head. "And that makes me fear the

worst. That Duncan may even be…" She didn't finish the sentence but he knew what she meant.

She was worried her brother was dead.

"It will work out," he assured her. "We'll keep Duncan in our prayers."

"That helps," she agreed.

He wanted to press for more, not understanding why her father wouldn't tell her what Duncan was doing. Especially since Ian seemed to know she and Brodie were in danger. Why else would he tell her to go back to Nashville? Still, he kept his doubts to himself.

"I will protect you and Brodie with my life," he promised, tucking a lock of hair behind her ear.

A reluctant smile played at the corner of her mouth. "I believe you."

He kissed her again, unable to stay away from her sweetness. She kissed him back, filling his heart with hope and anticipation. But then a soft crying from inside the cabin forced Mike to lift his head. "Is that Brodie?" he asked.

"Huh?" Shayla's smile faded as the words hit home. "Oh, yes. I better check on him."

She pulled away to go inside the cabin. He stayed where he was for a moment, trying to understand the myriad emotions tumbling through him.

The way she'd kissed him had reminded him of better times. He savored the closeness and thought there was a good possibility that they'd be able to recapture the love they'd once shared.

He entered the cabin and made his way over to the doorway of Shayla and Brodie's room. The boy's sobs had quieted, but Shayla continued to rock him back and forth, whispering reassurances that he would be fine and that she would stay with him for the rest of the night.

Watching them, he wished he had the ability to hold Brodie close, to battle the nightmares the day's gunfire had brought on.

Maybe someday…

Retreating from the doorway, he moved his box of notes back onto the table and then sat to work. Knowing his family would descend upon them tomorrow meant that he needed to get his thoughts together tonight.

He wanted to present a tight theory of his father's case to his siblings. Unfortunately the threads were convoluted and tangled, which left him with holes in the overall picture.

Following up on Donte Parkerside's untimely death was the most likely place to start. He'd paid a fee to get access to the police report that provided scant information. The victim had been seated on the front porch of his house when the occupants of a dark-colored sports car fired several shots at him. Parkerside had taken two bullets in the chest and was pronounced dead at the scene.

Three witnesses were interviewed. One claimed the car was black. Another said it was dark green. The third said it was blue. None of the witnesses could recall a license plate number or describe any of the occupants inside the vehicle.

The location of the drive-by shooting was only a couple of blocks from where Elliot had been shot. Which didn't prove anything other than that Elliot and Parkerside both lived in the area. Not surprising since they'd clearly been hanging out together.

Another dead end, Mike thought with a sigh.

Scrolling down the report, his gaze snagged on the name of the officer who'd taken the report.

Rafe Scarletti.

Mike straightened in his seat, his pulse racing. The same cop who'd shot Curt Elliot had taken the report on Parkerside's murder?

A coincidence? Maybe. Cops were assigned to specific districts so it wasn't unusual that Scarletti would be working in the area the night of Parkerside's drive-by shooting.

But Mike wasn't buying it. He turned back to the report of the officer-involved shooting of Elliot. The time of Elliot's death was roughly ten thirty at night. Not too far from the normal change between the evening and graveyard shifts.

Turning back to the drive-by shooting—the time of Parkerside's death had been ten fifteen at night.

Goose bumps rippled over his skin.

Was Scarletti working for the Dark Knights?

Mike pulled up a new document on his computer screen and began a fresh timeline, starting with Lindsey Baker's injury, then Elliot's shooting, along with his father's murder shortly thereafter. He ended the timeline with Parkerside's death by an alleged drive-by shooter.

When finished, Mike created a second timeline that included all the most recent events. He started with the night he'd witnessed Duncan O'Hare meeting with Lane Walters, followed by the drive-by shooting attempt on Shayla and Brodie outside Duncan's home. He ended with the most recent gunfire that had occurred at Hawk's cabin.

Reviewing the dual timelines, he found it interesting that Peter Fresno's name hadn't come up, other than as Duncan's partner. The antagonistic vibe he'd got from Fresno still bothered him. Maybe Duncan was working undercover, but Fresno wasn't aware of his partner's activities. If Fresno didn't trust Duncan O'Hare, it would make sense that he'd be less than cooperative when being questioned.

Or maybe Fresno just didn't like being partnered with the chief's son.

And his search on Ryker Tillman, Duncan's old buddy from the academy, hadn't given him anything, either. The guy's address and phone were unlisted and Mike made a note to ask Miles or Matt to find the cop's contact information.

The parallels between the two timelines were obvious. The same tactic of a drive-by shooting used on Parkerside had been repeated with the attack on Shayla and Brodie. But after that, the two timelines diverged.

The black sports car had taken shots at Shayla and Brodie, not just once, but four times. He stared at his notes for a long moment. Why had the same tactic been used so often? Ridiculous for anyone to believe a random shooting had occurred four times in as many days.

It didn't make any sense.

He began researching other drive-by shootings and found three more in roughly the same neighborhood where Elliot's and Parkerside's deaths had occurred.

Writing the names of those three victims down, he began to investigate each and every one.

When he finished, he stared at the results. Only one of the victims, a woman by the name of Angelica Corbin, had been investigated by Rafe Scarletti. The same cop and the same time frame of between ten and ten thirty at night. The other two had different officers' names.

Digging deeper, he discovered that Angelica Corbin had been accused of harming a child under her care, but the child's death had been ruled accidental. Corbin had been out on bail, only to be gunned down by a random shooter less than two weeks later.

Mike added her to the list of Dark Knights' victims because she certainly fitted the pattern. He didn't agree with the Dark Knights taking the law into their own hands, acting as judge and jury by outright killing people who were likely guilty of committing heinous crimes.

Yet in a way he could understand the motivation behind

the murders. It couldn't be easy to work in law enforcement, putting your life on the line to put the bad guys behind bars only to have them released onto the street a short time later. But that was the way the system worked. The balance of justice offered everyone the fair treatment of being considered innocent until proved guilty.

What made him the most upset was that the Dark Knights hadn't only taken down criminals. That was bad enough. But they'd crossed the line. The power they held must have gone to their heads because they hadn't balked at killing an innocent man.

His father.

And now they were going even further by trying to kill an innocent woman and her child.

The type of people they'd claimed to be vindicating by their actions. Their intention of making the streets safe for the public to go out after dark had been shoved to the wayside.

Now their goal appeared to be to keep their activities a secret at all costs.

At midnight, Mike couldn't keep his eyes open, so he locked up the cabin and stretched out on the sofa.

Just before sleep claimed him, he felt a deep certainty that he would soon know the truth about his father's murder.

Bringing badly needed justice and closure to the Callahan clan.

Shayla woke early the next morning with a crick in her neck. She'd fallen asleep next to Brodie, and thankfully he hadn't experienced any more nightmares.

Stretching out her neck muscles with a low groan, she washed up in the bathroom, then headed into the kitchen to make coffee. When the coffee was finished, she filled a mug and took a grateful sip. She carried it to the table and pushed aside a pile of papers to make room.

The computer screen flashed, revealing a document on the page. Leaning forward, she was stunned to see the timeline of recent events involving her and Brodie laid out in an objective format.

It felt creepy to read every detail about what had transpired, including the date, time and location.

"Good morning."

Mike's voice startled her. Hot coffee sloshed over the rim of her mug, burning her hand. Feeling guilty, as if she'd infringed on his privacy, she turned toward him. He was sitting on the sofa, rubbing his hands over his face.

"Oh, I, uh, didn't see you there." Why on earth had he slept on the couch? She hastily rose. "Would you like some coffee?"

"That would be wonderful." Mike joined her in the kitchen, leaning his hip against the counter as he accepted the mug from her hands. "Thanks."

"You're welcome." He looked so attractive standing there, it was hard to focus. "I can make breakfast if you need to keep working."

"What did you think of the timeline?" he asked.

She stared at him. "I don't know how to answer that. It was strange to read about it as if it happened to someone else."

He nodded, his expression thoughtful. "I can see that. But it helps me to have it down in factual black-and-white terms."

"That makes sense." She took another sip of her coffee. "I changed my mind," she said, abruptly changing the subject.

"About what?"

She drew in a deep breath and looked him directly in the eye. "About going to visit my dad. It's too risky.

I wouldn't be able to stand knowing I somehow brought danger to the hospital."

"I see." Mike's gaze was difficult to read.

"After the phone call last night, I decided not to go," she added, feeling the need to explain herself.

There was a long pause before he nodded. "Okay, that's fine."

"Good." She smiled in relief. "Matt brought eggs, so I'll get started. Brodie likes scrambled eggs and toast."

"Brodie seems to like all food," Mike said dryly. "I thought most kids, like my niece Abby, were very picky eaters."

"I hear that a lot from his teachers at his pre-K program," she admitted, pulling the eggs and the milk out of the fridge. "I count my blessings that I don't have to worry about him not eating enough nutritious food."

Mike grinned. One of the disposable phones on the counter began to vibrate. He scooped it up before she could. "Hello?"

She couldn't hear who was on the other side of the line, but figured it had to be Matt as he was the only one who would have had the number.

"You can head up here anytime," Mike confirmed. "But you might want to bring food for lunch. We don't have enough here to feed everyone."

For some reason she was nervous about seeing the rest of Mike's siblings. She'd met them before, but having Brodie, she knew it was only a matter of time before they figured out the boy was Mike's son.

They were all Christians and she couldn't help but wonder if they would look down at her for being a single mother. For having a child outside marriage. She had no idea if they knew Mike had proposed the morning after their one night together, before he'd known about Brodie, and that she'd accepted.

Their six-day engagement had to be the shortest one in history.

She stared down at her ringless left hand, remembering how he'd promised to buy her an engagement ring.

"Mommy?" Brodie's voice from the bedroom doorway had her turning to him.

"Good morning. Let's go to the bathroom. Breakfast will be ready soon, okay?"

"I'll take over," Mike said, disconnecting from the call. "Matt and the rest of the gang will be heading out shortly. Maddy and Noah have a few errands to do first, but they've promised to bring lunch."

"Sounds good," she said, ignoring the knots in her stomach at the prospect of seeing all his siblings at the same time in one place. "Come on, Brodie."

She made sure Brodie washed up and brushed his teeth before going out to the kitchen for breakfast. Her son eagerly scrambled up onto his chair as Mike finished the eggs and buttered the toast.

"Wait, Brodie," she said as Mike set their plates on the table. "We have to pray first."

Brodie let out a sigh, but allowed her to hold his hand. When he readily reached for Mike's hand, too, she smiled.

This was how it should be. All of them together, praying before their meal.

Was she wrong to dream of this for their future? She bowed her head, telling herself to leave it in God's hands.

"Dear Lord, we ask that You bless this food we are about to eat. We thank You for keeping us and our families safe in Your care. We ask that You please guide us on Your chosen path today. Amen."

"Amen," she and Brodie said at the same time.

"Dig in," Mike said to Brodie.

The little boy grinned and picked up his spoon to eat his scrambled eggs.

When they'd finished eating, Shayla busied herself with cleanup duties. Brodie played on the living room floor with his plastic cars, one eye on the cartoons on the television set. She'd just finished putting away the last of the dishes when Matt's SUV pulled up to the front of the cabin.

Through the window she saw three of Mike's brothers get out of the vehicle. Matt opened the back latch and Duchess jumped out. The Callahans all came toward the cabin. Her stomach did a little flip-flop as she dried her hands on a dish towel and went over to open the door.

"Come in," she invited.

"Thanks." Matt and Duchess came in first, followed by Mitch, who was about Mike's size but with blond hair. Marc followed, his expression serious as he nodded at her.

"Shayla, you remember my brothers—Marc, Mitch and, of course, Matt."

"Of course. Nice to see you again." She twisted the towel nervously in her hand. "That's my son, Brodie."

Marc and Mitch glanced at the boy, their gazes curious. Duchess went over to lick Brodie, sending him into a fit of giggles. The knots in Shayla's stomach tightened, but none of the brothers asked the obvious question about Brodie's father.

"Hey, is that my file folder?" Marc asked, pulling a black folder out of the box. "I've been looking all over for it!"

"Those are my blueprints, too," Mitch exclaimed. "Where did you get them?"

Mike raised his hands in a show of surrender. "Okay. Look, I know what I did was wrong and I'm sorry. I shouldn't have taken your notes and blueprints without your knowledge. But let's look on the bright side. The fact that I borrowed them is the only reason we have everything right here at our fingertips."

Marc lightly punched Mike on the shoulder. "You have some nerve, bro."

"Doesn't he?" Mitch echoed with a scowl. "The only reason I'm not punching you is because you helped me out of a jam last summer. Consider us even."

Marc grimaced. "I guess you've helped us all out at one point or another. I take that punch back."

"You can't take it back," Mike protested, making a show of rubbing his shoulder. "Now that we've all agreed to move beyond this, let's get to work."

The four men sat at the table, Duchess stretched out on the floor at Matt's feet. Shayla made another pot of coffee for them, then decided it would be best to get Brodie out of their hair for a while.

"Would you like to play on the swing set?" she asked.

"Yeah!" Brodie readily abandoned his plastic cars. "I wanna swing!"

"Put the cars away first," she instructed him. "You don't want them to get broken, do you?"

Brodie looked as if he might argue but then nodded and gathered them into a small pile that he placed in the corner of the sofa.

"Good boy," she said, taking him by the hand. Duchess lifted her head, watching them, but didn't move from her position beside Matt. The Callahan brothers were in deep conversation as they pored over Mike's timelines, and didn't seem to notice as she led Brodie outside.

The sun wasn't very high in the sky at midmorning, but still warm on her skin. She pushed Brodie on his swing, then watched as he went down the slide over and over again.

"Swing again," he said, pulling on the chain.

Knowing there wasn't anything she could do to help the

men inside, she obliged him by lifting him into her arms. Before she could set him on the seat of the swing, she felt someone come up behind her.

Expecting another Callahan sibling, she turned. When she saw the stranger with a gun in his hand, she froze.

"What—" she began but stopped when he shoved the nose of the gun firmly into her side.

"Don't say a word," he warned. "Or I'll shoot you both right here and take my chances."

She tightened her grip on Brodie, hoping and praying that Mike or someone else from the house would look out the window.

But they didn't.

"This way." The stranger with the gun urged her toward the path she'd gone down the night before.

She tried to drag her feet, but the gunman's response was to poke her harder with the weapon. She thought she heard Duchess growl, but the sound quickly faded away. The path wound through the trees and came out in another clearing where a dark sports car was parked. She could see there was a man in the driver's seat.

Two men against one woman and a three-year-old child. She was a little surprised neither one of them was Peter Fresno.

"Get in."

She didn't want to get in. She didn't want to go anywhere with these men. But disobeying wasn't an option. Not with the gun digging into her side.

No! Help us! Dear Lord, keep us safe!

FIFTEEN

"Rafe Scarletti, huh?" Marc said thoughtfully. "That's good detective work, bro. I don't think Scarletti has ever been flagged on our list."

"Your list?" Mike echoed in confusion. Then it hit him. "The FBI's list? The feds have been investigating the Dark Knights?"

Marc gave a brief nod. "Internal Affairs asked for our support."

Mike was dumbfounded by the news. "Local police departments never ask for help from the feds."

"I know." Marc shrugged. "But with all the concern across the country about officer-involved shootings, we've been working really closely with MPD's internal affairs. Personally, I'm glad they made an exception in this case."

"Was that before or after Dad's murder?" Matt asked.

"After," Marc acknowledged. "But the investigation didn't go very far. There wasn't enough evidence." Marc's smile was crooked. "Apparently we should have asked for assistance from a certain private investigator."

Mike was glad his brothers seemed to have forgiven him for taking their notes and evidence. "I missed identifying Scarletti the first time around. But I think he's our guy."

"Not just him," Mitch corrected. "Where there's one dirty cop, there're likely more."

Mike nodded. Mitch had a right to be wary after being framed by his own boss almost a year ago. Sometimes the people you trusted the most were the ones who stabbed you in the back. Mike glanced at his watch. "When do you think Noah and Maddy will get here?"

"Within the hour," Matt confirmed. "A little longer since they're planning to stop to pick up lunch for the group along the way."

"Sounds good." Mike turned his attention back to the investigation. "I think our next step should be to reach out to some of the top brass at MPD. Kirk Stoltz was always a good friend of our dad's. I think he would be our best choice to tap for inside information."

"We could also try Gordon Beecher," Matt added, leaning over to scratch Duchess behind the ears. "He's the chief's second-in-command. A neutral party might be helpful."

"Speaking of which," Mitch interrupted. "Didn't you date Shayla before Dad died? While you were still in the academy?"

Mike shifted in his seat, uncomfortable with the line of questioning and their meddling in his personal life. "Yes, but what does that have to do with anything? Stay focused, will you? Yeah, her father is the chief of police, but he's recuperating in the hospital from open-heart surgery. And her brother, Duncan, is in the wind."

Marc whistled under his breath. "That doesn't sound good."

"It's not." Mike gestured toward the second timeline. "As you can see, Duncan met with Lane Walters, the suspected leader of the Dark Knights, near the apartment building where Walters lives. It's possible Duncan is attempting to infiltrate the organization, working undercover for the MPD."

"Wait a minute." Mitch unrolled the blueprints of the two-story apartment building. "I remember looking at Walters. He lives in the corner apartment, here." He tapped the bottom right corner of the blueprint.

Mike leaned over to see what his brother was referring to. "Okay, that makes sense."

"No, you're missing the point. See this?" Mitch pointed to an opening with slash lines through them. "This is the only apartment in the building that has direct access to the basement. But what's really interesting is that there's another doorway from the basement leading outside, over here on the opposite side of the place." Mitch drew a line across the length of the building. "I remember thinking that this was how the shooter may have escaped the night of Dad's murder."

Mike stared. He'd taken Mitch's blueprints but had missed that key piece of information.

How many other important clues had he missed?

He'd been so incredibly stupid. And arrogant. This was exactly why cops often created a task force. Because having several different viewpoints while working on a case was far more valuable than one.

Guilt and regret washed over him. He never should have tried to investigate his father's murder on his own.

With a jerk, he shoved away from the table, needing distance from his brothers. He crossed over to the counter and filled his coffee mug, his thoughts whirling.

They'd got over him borrowing their notes, but he wasn't so sure he could forgive himself.

"Hey, Mike, remember Eddie Jarvis?" Matt asked. "He was in your academy graduating class, wasn't he?"

"Yeah." Mike pushed his emotional turmoil aside and turned to face his brother. "What about him?"

"He was partnered briefly with Scarletti," Matt said. "Guess who he's related to?"

"Who?" Mike said, growing irritated.

"Lane Walters. Apparently they're cousins on his mom's side of the family."

"Being related doesn't automatically make you a criminal," he protested, returning to the table to see what Matt had up on the computer screen.

"No, but it's a link. Something to add to your timeline."

"The threads are starting to come together," Marc agreed. "We absolutely have to take this to Kirk Stoltz or Gordon Beecher."

"Why not both?" Mitch asked. "What's the harm? The more people who know, the better chance we have of uncovering the truth."

"Maybe," Mike agreed. His instincts were to stick with the people who were personally involved with their father. "Let's start with Kirk Stoltz. Remember how upset he was at Dad's funeral? He's the one more likely to bend a few rules to find justice for Dad."

"That's true," Matt agreed. Duchess started growling low in her throat and he silenced her with a stern look. "I'm with you, Mike. Let's do it."

Duchess began to growl again, her dark gaze seemingly locked on the cabin door.

"What's wrong, Dutch?" Matt asked.

"Maybe she wants to go out to play with Brodie." Mike peered out the window, expecting to see Shayla and Brodie near the swing set. But there was no sign of them. "That's weird."

"What?" Matt asked.

Fear gnawed at him. Mike strode toward the door.

"They're not on the playground. Give me a minute to track them down."

"We'll take Duchess with us," Matt said, jumping to his feet.

"Let's all go." Mitch flanked Mike on one side while Marc joined them.

The clearing outside the cabin was empty. One of the swings swayed back and forth in the breeze, but there was no sign of other cabin renters around, either.

"Shayla! Brodie!" Mike shouted, hearing the lonely echo of his voice reflecting back at him. "Where are you?"

There was no response.

"Where are they?" Mike asked, frustration lacing his tone. "If she took a walk without telling me..." His voice trailed off as he realized Shayla wouldn't do that.

Not with Brodie.

"Something's wrong," he said, turning to his brothers. "Something has happened to them."

"Easy now, don't panic," Marc warned.

"Why don't you get something of Shayla's?" Matt suggested. "Duchess can track her scent."

"Good idea." Mike didn't waste any time but hurried inside, returning with Shayla's sweater. "Try this."

Matt held the sweater up to his K-9's nose. "Find, Duchess," he ordered. "Find!"

Duchess dropped her nose to the ground and began making circles near the swing set, alerting at Shayla's scent.

"Good girl," Matt praised. "Find!"

Duchess moved in what appeared to be a random pattern, but eventually made her way toward the path Shayla had taken the night before. Mike's hopes plummeted. Duchess had obviously picked up Shayla's scent from yesterday.

But the dog continued down the path, sniffing and circling, sitting and then going down the path again. When Duchess continued past the cluster of trees Shayla had stopped at the night before, Mike was filled with renewed hope.

The K-9 led them to a clearing. Duchess made another circle and then sat, alerting at Shayla's scent.

"Good girl," Matt praised again. "Find!"

Duchess didn't move. Mike felt sick as he approached the area.

"Tire tracks," he said in a hoarse voice.

Marc came over and knelt beside the imprint. "They look fresh, but there's no way to say for sure."

"Except that Duchess followed Shayla's scent here and then lost it." Mike lifted his tortured gaze to his brother's, knowing deep in his heart that he'd failed in his promise to keep them safe.

"Shayla and Brodie have been kidnapped."

Battling panic, Shayla held Brodie close, trying to comfort him as he cried against her. She told herself to focus on the highway signs, keeping track of the route they were taking. She also tried to catch the eyes of other drivers, thinking she could somehow signal distress, but there wasn't that much traffic on the roads and no one in the vehicles around them paid any attention.

She hoped that maybe a cop would notice that Brodie wasn't in a child safety seat and pull them over. Unfortunately she didn't see any law enforcement vehicles as they headed into Milwaukee.

"Where are you taking us?" she demanded, trying to sound confident instead of scared to death.

Both the driver and the man with the gun ignored her.

"Did you hear me?" She swallowed hard, trying not

to show the extent of her fear. "I want to know where you're taking us!"

"Silence," the gunman barked.

Brodie's sobs increased in volume and she quickly turned her attention to soothing her son. "Shh, Brodie. It's okay. Don't cry, we're going to be okay."

"I wanna go home," Brodie sobbed.

"I know." She couldn't bear to think about the fact that they may never get back to Nashville.

That they may not survive the day. After all, these were the same men who'd tried to shoot her several times over. What would stop them from pulling over into some remote location and killing her and Brodie outright?

No! She didn't want to die!

Fear and desperation clawed at her throat, threatening to overwhelm her. She knew she needed to stay strong for Brodie, but it was hard to think about anything other than the dire fate that awaited them.

She'd never felt so helpless in her entire life.

"Brodie, let's pray, okay? The way Daddy taught us to."

Brodie continued to cry.

"Dear Lord," she said out loud, a tremor in her tone. "We ask You to keep us safe in Your care. We ask You to steer these two men away from evil and encourage them to show mercy on us. Heavenly Father, if we are to die today at the hands of these men, please bring us up to live with You in Heaven. We ask this in Your name. Amen."

The gunman shifted uncomfortably in his seat, but the gun he pointed at her didn't waver. She wasn't sure that her prayer would change his intentions on what to do with them, but it couldn't hurt.

"Please, Lord, keep us safe in Your care," she repeated, determined to find a way to get through to these men. "Come on, Brodie, pray with me," she urged. "Lord God, we ask that You steer these men away from their evil path and show them the light of goodness—"

"Knock it off," the gunman abruptly growled in a threatening tone. "Shut up or I'll shoot you both here and now."

She didn't dare look at him, but kept her head bowed over her son. Instead of stopping, she simply lowered her voice to a whisper, her mouth near Brodie's ear. "God is watching over us, Brodie. He'll protect us and keep us safe."

"Amen," Brodie whispered in response to the prayer.

Instantly she felt a sense of calm wash over her. She and Brodie were not alone in the car with these men. God was with them. Maybe they would survive this or maybe they wouldn't. But they'd never be alone. And she held fast to the belief that Mike and the rest of the Callahans would find her and Brodie before it was too late.

The gunman didn't say anything else, avoiding her gaze. Another fifteen minutes passed in complete silence and when she felt the vehicle slow down, she glanced over to take note they were leaving the interstate.

Keeping up with the street signs proved futile. Some she recognized, but others she didn't, which wasn't a surprise considering she'd been away from Milwaukee for the past four years.

The neighborhood around them grew more run-down and she suppressed a shiver.

Being in this area of the city didn't bode well for what they might face when they reached their final destination. And the more time that passed since she and Brodie had left the playground outside the cabin, the less likely it would be that Mike would find them.

Brodie shifted against her. Something hard pressed

along her right side and she belatedly realized that she still had one of the disposable phones.

Hope flickered in her chest, her mind racing with possibilities. She absolutely couldn't afford for these men to search her and find it. Her right side was near the passenger door and she subtly moved her right arm from Brodie, trying to figure out a way to get to the phone deep in the pocket of her hooded sweatshirt.

The vehicle slowed again, the driver taking a sharp right turn. The movement shifted her to the left and she quickly wrapped both arms around Brodie to keep him firmly against her.

She inwardly groaned when the driver pulled into the parking lot tucked behind an apartment building. She was running out of time!

Why hadn't she thought of the phone sooner?

The vehicle stopped and the gunman held the gun on her while the driver slid out from behind the wheel. Then he gestured at her with the weapon. "Get out, slowly. You try to run or scream and I will shoot you and the kid, too."

She nodded, although she couldn't help thinking he was bluffing. A gunshot in the middle of the city, even in an area with high crime rates, would still attract attention.

But then the driver pulled open her door and stood there, waiting for her to get out. Praying they wouldn't find her phone, she awkwardly shifted in the seat, swinging her legs over so she could get out of the car while still holding Brodie.

"This way," the gunman said as he joined them.

She glanced around looking for someone who might help her, but the couple of kids huddled at the corner of the parking lot didn't bother to glance in her direction.

Hitching Brodie higher in her arms, she followed the driver into the apartment building. The place smelled of stale cigarette smoke and grease, causing her stomach to roll with nausea. But then the driver opened another door, revealing a set of wooden stairs leading into a dank, dark basement.

"Go," the gunman said, prodding her with his gun.

Taking the steep staircase down while holding Brodie wasn't easy. She used the rail beneath her right elbow as a guide, wondering if the two men were hoping she'd fall and hit her head on the concrete basement floor below.

How she managed to negotiate the stairs all the way down was a mystery. The darkness caused Brodie to whimper. She stood at the bottom of the stairs, giving her eyes a minute to adjust to the lack of light.

"In here," the man with the gun said.

There must have been a window down there somewhere, as she could tell he was standing near a door. He fiddled with it for a moment, then opened the door and gestured for her to go inside. The moment she stepped over the threshold, he slammed the door shut behind her.

Hearing a jiggling and metallic clink of the door handle, she felt certain he was locking them inside. The faint light of the window vanished, leaving them swallowed in darkness. Shayla stood frozen, afraid to move, uncertain as to what if anything was inside.

"I'm scared. Turn on the light," Brodie whispered.

"Don't be afraid. We're safe for now." She ran her fingers over the wall near the door, feeling rough drywall. "I'm not sure if there is a light down here, sorry."

A low moan cut the silence and she froze again, feeling sick as she realized they were not alone.

"Who's in here?" she demanded, huddling with Brodie against the wall.

"Shay?"

At first she thought she imagined the faint husky voice, but then he spoke again. "Shay? Is that you?"

"Duncan?" She wished desperately for even a sliver of light.

"Yeah." He groaned again and she heard him moving around. "I, uh, can't get up."

The brief flood of relief at not being alone quickly faded. "Why not?"

"They, uh, busted me up some."

"Oh, Duncan." With one arm circling Brodie, she used the other to follow the wall until she found Duncan. He was curled up on the floor near the back of the room. She knelt beside him, running her fingers over his face and feeling the puffy skin and the stickiness of blood.

Knowing these men had beaten up her brother in an effort to get him to talk infuriated and scared her.

They were prisoners. And she knew that if any of the men who'd kidnapped them raised a hand to her son, she'd tell them whatever they wanted to know.

Anything.

SIXTEEN

They were gone. Taken from the playground. *Gone!*

Mike couldn't concentrate on the case, his thoughts kept going around and around, emphasizing his failure.

Shayla. Their son. Both in the hands of cold-blooded killers.

"Mike!" His brother Matt roughly shook his arm. "Snap out of it, bro. We need to work together to find them."

"I know." He lifted tortured eyes to his brothers. "How? What's our next step?"

There was a long moment of silence as they considered their options.

"I say we go to Lane Walters's apartment building," Marc said. "We can ask Miles and Noah to meet us there."

"We need a search warrant," Matt pointed out.

Mike couldn't have cared less about going through formal channels. The woman he loved—yes, *loved*—and their son were in danger. That trumped a warrant any day of the week.

"Call Maddy," Marc suggested. "She'll know which judge to approach to get the warrant."

"I don't need one," Mike said, lifting his chin and staring down his brothers. "As a private investigator, I'm not held to the same rules."

Matt put a hand on his arm. "Mike, listen to me. We can't hold Walters or anyone else responsible for Dad's murder unless we go through the proper channels. Without a search warrant, the DA will throw out any evidence we find and they'll get off scot-free. We can't let them get away with this."

"And in the meantime?" Mike didn't care how upset he sounded. "I'm just supposed to wait while you guys jump through circus hoops, leaving Shayla and Brodie in danger?"

"I'll take him to the apartment building," Mitch offered. "He can sneak in while you guys get the paperwork you need."

"And if Shayla and Brodie aren't there, then what?" Marc's face was flushed with anger. "You can't botch this up for us, Mike. We don't know where they're being held. They could be anywhere."

Mike knew his eldest brother was right, but that was all the more reason they needed to move quickly. To eliminate one potential hiding place before moving to another.

"I think we should split up, as Mitch suggested," Mike said. "We'll take the apartment building. Marc, you should call Miles so the two of you can head over to speak with Gordon Beecher, the second in command. If he's not available, go to Kirk Stoltz. We need someone high up in authority on this. Maybe Matt and Duchess could go to Peter Fresno's place. Duchess would be able to search for Shayla's scent."

"What about Noah?" Matt asked.

Mike thought about it for a moment. "Send him to confront Rafe Scarletti. If he knows we're onto him, he might talk in exchange for a lighter sentence."

Marc threw up his hands in frustration. "But we don't have anything on him! No solid proof against *anyone*."

Mike took a threatening step toward his brother. "And if it was Kari, Maggie and Max who'd been kidnapped? Would you feel the same way?"

Marc let out a heavy sigh at the reference to his wife and two children, named in honor of their parents. "No," he roughly admitted. "I wouldn't."

"Okay, then. It's settled." Mike turned to Mitch. "Let's get cracking."

They strode quickly back to the cabin in silence. Mike had no idea how they'd been found at the remote location, not that it mattered. The damage was done. They'd been found. Shayla and Brodie had been kidnapped.

Might even already be dead.

He didn't want to think about it, but the very real possibility nagged at him. The gunman had made so many attempts against her already, what was one more?

He couldn't imagine the gunman having a reason to wait.

As he opened the cabin door, his phone rang in his pocket. Surprised, he pulled it out and glanced at the screen. The number was almost identical to the one he was using.

Shayla!

He quickly answered, his heart pounding. "Hello?"

"M-Mike?" The connection was so bad, he could barely hear her through the static.

"Shayla? Where are you?"

"Base—ap—" Her voice continued to break up. "Dunc—"

He gripped the phone tightly. "I can't hear you. Can you speak up? Are you with Duncan?"

"Hurry" was all he heard before the line went dead.

"What did she say?" Marc asked.

"The connection was terrible, I couldn't make out most of it. She mentioned 'base ap' and 'Duncan.'"

"Basement of an apartment building?" Mitch asked. "Phones don't work well when surrounded by concrete."

Relief at his brother's brilliance washed over him. "Yes, that must be it."

"And that's more than enough for a warrant," Marc said in satisfaction. "I don't even need Maddy's connection. With a statement from the victim herself, I can get a warrant from the FBI."

What Mike had heard was more garbled than statement but he wasn't about to argue. Especially since he didn't even want to wait that long. But knowing Shayla was alive helped keep him calm. "Can you get it on the way?"

"Yeah." Marc already had his phone to his ear. His eldest brother took a few steps away, speaking rapidly to the person on the other end of the line.

"Why can't he call from the car?" Mike asked, chafing at the wait. "We should already be on the road by now."

"I think he's arranging backup," Mitch said. "We can't just go in guns blazing. Not when we have no idea what we're facing."

He hated to admit his brother was right. But standing around was driving him nuts. He picked up his phone and called the number for MPD station one, asking to be connected to Kirk Stoltz. Gordon Beecher might be the proper channel, but he intended to get his father's friend on board, as well.

"One moment, please."

Annoying music played in the background while he waited for his father's friend to pick up.

"Stoltz," a deep voice finally answered.

"This is Mike Callahan," he quickly identified himself. "I need your help. We believe we've identified the cops who are linked to the Dark Knights."

"Really?" Stoltz's voice rose with excitement. "Tell me!"

For some reason Mike hesitated. "I will, but we need to meet in person. I'm going to ask Miles to catch up with you, okay? And I need you to help smooth the way on this. We don't have a lot of time."

"Of course. I'm happy to talk to Miles. But why be so evasive? I need to know what evidence you have so we can move on this immediately."

He glanced over to see that Mitch had the blueprints to the apartment buildings under his arm as he headed for his SUV. "Rafe Scarletti," Mike said. "That's the name we have, although there are some others. I have to go. Watch for Miles, okay?"

"Absolutely. And, Mike? Be careful."

"We will." Mike disconnected and jogged to catch up with Mitch.

"I've got the warrant," Marc said with grim satisfaction, holding up his smartphone. "It's a scanned document for now, but should be good enough to get inside."

"Good." That was all Mike needed to know. He slid into the back seat, leaving Mitch and Marc up front. While they'd waited for the warrant, Matt had loaded Duchess into the back of his SUV and was already heading for the highway, getting a nice head start toward Fresno's place.

Mike called Miles, filling him in on the upcoming meeting with Stoltz. Miles didn't hesitate to agree.

When he finished with that call, he called Hawk. His buddy had already gone out on a limb for him, but Mike wasn't above asking for yet another favor. Hawk readily agreed to meet them downtown. Lastly, he tried Shayla again. But the phone went straight to a message that informed him the device was not set up to accept messages.

Had she run out of battery? Or had she simply turned the phone off because the reception was so awful?

Tapping his foot impatiently, he strove for patience. And lifted his heart in prayer.

Please, Lord, keep Shayla and Brodie safe! Guide me so that I find them before it's too late!

Shayla huddled next to Duncan with Brodie sitting on her lap, feeling reassured by both her brother's presence and that her phone call to Mike had gone through. At least, she was pretty sure it had. It had been difficult to hear with all the static on the line.

Brodie had finally fallen asleep. She was glad he was able to get some rest, and giving him what was left of the fish crackers in her pocket may have helped.

She hoped and prayed that this wouldn't traumatize her little boy forever.

"You're sure Callahan will come?" Duncan rasped.

"I'm sure." Duncan knew Brodie was Mike's son. "He suspected you of being with the Dark Knights, though. Did you and Dad really discuss them at the funeral?"

"Yeah," Duncan admitted. "But only because we'd heard about one of the victims attempting to commit suicide. A young woman confined to a wheelchair tried to kill herself. We didn't condone what they were doing, but there was a part of their mission that made sense."

That explained a lot, Shayla thought. "Why did they go after you?" she asked.

There was a slight hesitation before he answered.

"Dad asked me to infiltrate the Dark Knights by working undercover. I set up a meeting with Lane Walters and convinced him I wanted in on the deal. I told him how Dad and I didn't see eye to eye any longer and I was fed up with the never-ending bureaucracy.

"Walters seemed happy to have me on board at first, but Fresno was really mad. He kept railing at Walters that I was too much of a risk. He saw us together at the hospital—remember the first day we went to see Dad?

The day we learned he needed open-heart surgery? I tried to act as if I didn't care, but Fresno didn't buy it. Pete convinced Walters that I was working undercover to sniff out the dirty cops and had to be silenced."

She cast her memory back to the day Duncan referenced. "He was the guy in the car? The one you went over to talk to?"

"Yeah. I tried to convince Pete that I was putting on a front for you and Dad, but he didn't believe me. We'd been partners for a while, but had never got along, which was part of it. Plus he couldn't get over that my father was the chief of police. I didn't have much leverage to use to convince him to believe in me, although I made up a story about a girlfriend who'd been murdered and the guy who'd done it had got away with it."

"Did that really happen?"

He shrugged. "Yeah, which made it a good cover story, but Fresno wouldn't buy it. After Fresno saw us together that day, everything blew up in my face. I believe since you saw him there, he decided you had to be killed, too. He must have thought I'd confided in you about being undercover."

Fresno had been the gunman chasing her all over town, seemingly one step behind their every move? The news was mind-boggling. That he'd come after her and Brodie because of a mere suspicion was insane.

Then again, everything the Dark Knights did was crazy and irrational. Taking the law into their own hands, taking on the role of judge and jury. Killing people because of suspicions rather than proof.

"How did you get away from the Rustic Resort?"

"I left on foot. Dug down into the dirt of the farmer's field, lying flat against the ground, partially covered in soil. I saw you and Callahan pull up and almost came out of hiding, but I'm glad I didn't. I was there when the sports car came up behind you and began shooting. I suspected the driver was Fresno, but didn't have proof. I was relieved when you and Callahan managed to get away."

"You should have come out and joined us," she chided. "We would have been safer together."

"I almost did," he admitted. "But I didn't want to bring danger to you and Brodie. I figured it would be better if we stayed separated. I remained in the field most of the night. I eventually walked back to the motel, but the next day, Fresno found me. I've been his prisoner ever since."

She wasn't sure what to say. Knowing that she and Duncan had been so close that night was painful. If they'd been able to find each other, things may have turned out differently.

Especially since they were being held prisoners, despite Duncan's attempt to protect her.

The metallic clicking sound outside the door shot her pulse into the stratosphere.

They're back!

She felt Duncan stiffen beside her and knew he'd heard the noises, too. And then the door was opened, revealing a sliver of dim light.

"Get up. We need to leave."

No! She didn't want to leave! Not when she'd told Mike where to find them.

"Now!" The voice was rough with anger.

Brodie woke up and began to cry.

"Shh, it's okay, Brodie. We're okay." She staggered to her feet, using the cold cement wall for leverage so she wouldn't have to set Brodie down. She heard Duncan's labored breathing as he struggled to his feet.

The same two men stood on either side of the door, both holding guns pointed at them. Duncan was in no shape to fight them. She thought for sure that one of his eyes had swollen shut from the beating he'd suffered. Plus, she suspected he'd sustained a couple of cracked ribs.

She turned automatically to go up the basement stairs, but the gunman to her left roughly grabbed her arm.

"This way," he said harshly, pushing her forward. There wasn't much light and she battled a wave of helplessness, wondering if they were being led to the wall where they might be shot execution-style.

But they walked across the cold, damp, basement floor that seemed to go on forever. Then she saw a doorway.

"Open it," the gunman to her left demanded. He was the same one who'd done most of the talking while she and Brodie were being brought here.

She turned the knob and the door readily opened, revealing yet another staircase leading upward. Light illuminated the top of the stairs so she didn't hesitate to take them up to the main level.

The light should have been welcoming but it wasn't. Instead there were two more men with guns standing there. She recognized one of them as Duncan's partner, Peter Fresno.

"You," she croaked, blinking to bring his features into focus in the harsh daylight. Amazingly they were outside, not inside the apartment building at all.

"Shut up," he said, lifting his gun. "I should have taken care of you and Callahan when you came to my house, then we wouldn't be stuck dealing with you now."

"Knock it off," the other gunman said. "We need to move fast. The others are already here and the boss wants everyone together."

Others? A chill rippled over her. What others? The rest of the Callahans? Had they all been captured?

She bit her lip to keep from screaming at these lunatics to let them go.

"This way," the gunman to her left said, giving her a nudge with the tip of his weapon.

Gritting her teeth, she turned in the direction he indicated. Surprisingly they didn't go far, but straight to the apartment building right next door. A mirror image of the one they'd just left, down to the identical door leading into another cold, dark basement.

Defeat was staggering. Would Mike figure out to look for her and Brodie here? Or was it already too late? She didn't want to believe he'd been captured, but the words the gunman had spoken rang in her ears.

The others are already here and the boss wants everyone together.

Steeling herself for the worst, she carefully negotiated her and Brodie down the steep staircase. She could hear Duncan struggling behind her, his breath coming in short, fast pants. She hated knowing how much pain her brother was in and wished there was something she could do to get them out of there.

But there wasn't.

At the bottom of the basement stairs, she stood, waiting for direction. Her brother soon joined her, followed by all four of the gunmen.

Four of them, she thought desperately. Even if Mike hadn't been captured, how would they manage to get past four gunmen?

"Move," the man said gruffly from behind her.

She didn't wait to be prodded by the gun, but quickly walked forward, assuming the setup in this building was a mirror image of the other.

And she was right. At the other end of the long basement was a door with a padlock on the outside.

A man brushed past her and went to work unlocking the door. He swung it open and she shifted Brodie in her arms as she crossed the threshold.

"Who's there?" a querulous woman's voice asked. "My sons aren't going to rest until they find us, you hear me?"

Another, older female voice chimed in. "If you're smart, you'll let us go before they arrive."

"Shut up," the man beside her roared.

"Calm down, Jarvis," an older male voice said, stepping out from the corner of the basement. "After all, enticing the Callahans to come here is part of my master plan."

Shayla filed away the name Jarvis in the recesses of her memory even as she tried to understand what was going on. Who were the women inside the room? And why was getting the Callahans here part of the older man's master plan?

"Who is that?" the older female voice demanded.

There was a long moment of silence before the man named Jarvis broke it. "Get inside. Now!"

Shayla entered the room, heading toward the wall to allow space for Duncan to follow her.

The door clanged shut behind them and she could hear the metallic sound of the padlock being connected.

"Who's there?" the younger woman's tremulous voice asked.

"I'm Shayla O'Hare and I have my son, Brodie, and my brother, Duncan, with me, too." She hesitated and then added, "Who are you?"

"My name is Margaret Callahan and I have my mother, Eleanor with me, as well."

"My grandsons call me Nan," the shaky voice added.

Mike's mother and grandmother had been kidnapped, too? How was that possible?

Then she realized the truth. This was a trap in which she, Brodie, Mike's mother and grandmother were being used as bait.

SEVENTEEN

Mike's phone rang. He quickly answered it. "Hello?"

"Mike?" His sister Maddy's voice was thick with tears. "Something terrible has happened. Mom and Nan are gone."

A chill rippled over his skin. "What do you mean gone?"

"There are signs of a struggle at the house, chairs knocked over and spilled food on the counter. You know how Mom and Nan are total neat freaks. They're gone. Mom and Nan are gone!"

His stomach knotted with fear and dread. This couldn't be happening. He glanced at Mitch, who was driving into town toward the apartment building, and knew he had to remain calm for his sister's sake. "Okay, Maddy, try to relax. Call the police. Have them work it up as a crime scene."

"I know I need to relax. Stress isn't good for the baby."

Baby? Noah hadn't said a word about his wife being pregnant. "No, it's not," he agreed.

"I already called the police," Maddy continued as if he hadn't spoken. "But waiting for trace evidence from their home, if there is any, will take too long. We need to move on this, before it's too late."

"I know." Mike thought fast. Why harm two older women? This all had to be related to his father's murder. They must be getting close to uncovering the truth. "Listen, Shayla and Brodie are missing, too. I've been keeping them safe from harm, but they've been kidnapped. It's possible they're all together."

"But why?" Maddy's voice reflected desperate bewilderment. "I don't understand."

"I'm not sure, either, but it's the only thing that makes sense. Stay close to Noah, understand? I don't want you or the baby in danger, too." It was bad enough that four people he loved dearly were in harm's way.

"He's coming to pick me up now." Maddy sniffled loudly. "Where are you?"

"Just have Noah take you someplace safe," he insisted. "I'm with Mitch. Marc and Miles are heading to MPD to talk to either Beecher or Stoltz. Matt and Duchess are checking out another angle. I have Hawk meeting us, as well. Trust me, we can handle it."

"We're coming, too," Maddy insisted.

"No!" Mike's voice rose with frustration. "Maddy, if you want to help, stay there and make sure the cops find some sort of evidence. There has to be a fingerprint, a hair or something. We're going to need it."

There was a long pause before she reluctantly agreed. "Okay."

"Good." The small wave of relief was quickly overshadowed by the very real fear that the situation was unraveling faster than he could find the threads to stop it. "I'll talk to you later."

He ended the call.

"That's not good," Mitch said from the driver's seat.

"I know." He dragged his palms over his face. Think. He needed to think! "I'll call Matt, he needs to know."

"Same with Marc and Miles," Mitch agreed.

"Yeah." He contacted Matt first, hoping his brother may have reached Fresno's place by now.

"I was just going to call you," Matt said. "Fresno's place is empty, and Duchess hasn't picked up Shayla's scent. But I found several small drops of blood on the back porch. I think he's involved with the Dark Knights."

"I agree." Mike hadn't trusted the guy from the first time he'd met him. The blood could very well be Duncan's. "But there's worse news. Maddy just called from the house. She found signs of a struggle, plus Mom and Nan are gone."

"Gone?" Matt's voice went tense. "The same way Shayla and Brodie went missing?"

"Yeah. I need you to meet us at Lane Walters's apartment building. It's our best lead and I'm thinking that maybe we'll find all three women and Brodie there."

"I hope you're right. Catch up with you soon." Matt quickly disconnected from the call.

He called Marc next to tell him the latest and he promised to call Miles. "I'm not going to meet with Beecher or Stoltz," he said. "We need all hands on deck with Mom and Nan being taken."

"Okay. Stoltz already knows we've stumbled across the truth. Maybe you can try to get a message to Beecher, as well."

"Will do," Marc agreed.

The rest of the drive into the city seemed to take forever. But when Mitch got within a few blocks of the side-by-side apartment buildings, he parked the SUV. "We need to go from here on foot."

"Okay." As Mike pushed open his door, Matt's SUV pulled up behind them. Matt and Duchess soon joined them.

"I'd like to take Duchess over first, see if she picks up

Shayla's scent," Matt said, holding the bag with Shayla's sweater inside. "Once she picks that up, I'll give you the signal and we can surround the building."

Mike wiped his damp hands on his jeans. "We need to be careful, or they may shoot the women."

"That's why I want to be sure Shayla's in there first," Matt pointed out. "Give me at least ten minutes, okay?"

"Okay." Mike glanced at Mitch, who also nodded.

"Let's review the blueprints while he's gone," Mitch said. He opened the back of the SUV and used the back surface as a table as he unrolled the blueprints. "This building here—" he tapped the page "—is the one Marc has the search warrant for."

There were two buildings side by side, but only one that belonged to Rainbow Springs, LLC, the corporation believed to be a front for the Dark Knights.

"What about this building?" Mike indicated the one next to it. "Who owns this one? Is there a way we can get inside there to set up some sort of surveillance?"

"I'm not sure. Do you have my notes?" Mitch dug around in the box they'd brought along. "Oh, yeah, here it is. The place is owned by a different corporation, Baker's Dozen, LLC."

"Baker's Dozen?" Mike frowned, wondering why the name sounded so familiar. "Wait a minute! The name of the nineteen-year-old who was shot by Donte Parkerside was Baker. Lindsey Baker."

"That's not a coincidence," Mitch said, pulling out his phone. "We need Marc to expand the search warrant to include both buildings."

Mike's nerves were wound so tight he feared he'd snap. Why hadn't he noticed that connection earlier? Why hadn't he uncovered the truth about the Dark Knights a long time ago?

Why, Lord? Why?

"Thanks, Marc." Mitch turned, his expression grim. "He's working on the expanded warrant, but Marc wasn't able to reach Gordon Beecher or Kirk Stoltz. He left messages for both of them."

Mike understood that meant the brass at MPD could easily take action against them for not going through proper channels.

His phone rang. "Yeah?"

"Mike? Duchess alerted on Shayla's scent outside both apartment buildings."

"Both of them?" His gaze collided with Mitch's. "They can't be holding her in both places."

"No, but they can move her from one place to the other." Matt's voice was soft and Mike guessed he was hiding out somewhere close by. "I believe she's being held in the second building rather than the one on the corner."

Mike tightened his grip on the phone, his mind racing. What if Mitch was wrong? Storming the wrong apartment building would put Shayla and Brodie, and possibly their mother and grandmother, at risk. They could be shot before they could find them.

He froze, paralyzed with fear.

"Mike?" Matt's soft voice barely penetrated his dire thoughts. "Duchess alerted in a narrow walkway between the two buildings. It makes sense to me that they were moved from one building to the other. I'm telling you— she's in the second one."

"Okay." Mike swallowed hard and forced himself to trust his brother. Trust his family. And to trust that God was watching over them.

They'd find a way to save Shayla, Brodie, Mom and Nan.

Or die trying.

* * *

The darkness wasn't nearly as overwhelming when they all huddled together. It didn't matter that they were basically strangers, the three women, Duncan and Brodie stayed together, drawing strength from each other.

"The boys will come for us," Mike's mother said softly.

"I know, but it's a trap," Shayla whispered. "We need to warn them. I have a phone, but the connection is terrible."

"Try again anyway," Mike's mom said. "I wish I had brought my phone."

"The stupid man who grabbed me tossed mine in the garbage." Nan sounded annoyed.

Shayla tried Mike's number again, smiling a bit as she realized the two Callahan matriarchs were doing their best to keep their fear at bay with their brave comments. She admired them. Turning on her phone, she waited for it to power up.

The battery indicator was red and there was only one bar signaling a poor connection.

"Shay?" Mike's voice in her ear made her want to cry.

"Stay away," she whispered. "It's a trap!"

"What? Can't—you."

She knew he couldn't hear her, just like the last time she'd tried to talk to him. "Your mom and Nan are here," she tried again, speaking slowly.

"Coming—don't—"

The phone battery chose that moment to die, as if seeking a signal through the concrete was too much for it. Dejected, she slid the useless device back into her pocket. "I'm pretty sure they're coming to find us," she finally said. "I only hope they don't get hurt. There are four gunmen by my count, and likely more."

There was a long moment of silence as the group digested that bit of information.

"Even if we told them to stay away, they wouldn't," Margaret said. "They are too much like their father."

Shayla knew Mike's mom was right, but it didn't make her feel any better.

"We'll pray," Nan said firmly. She felt the older woman's hand grasp hers. "Dear Lord, we ask You to keep the Callahans and the O'Hares safe as we fight the evil men who seek to harm us. Amen."

"Amen," Shayla and Margaret echoed.

Brodie had fallen asleep. Shayla wasn't sure her brother believed in the power of prayer, but she hoped that when, not if, they got out of this mess, he'd give God and faith a try.

She was thankful to Mike for showing her the way to the Lord.

Shayla didn't know how much time had passed, but a loud bang made her jump. Tightening her grip on Brodie, she surged to her feet, fearing the worst.

Another loud bang was followed by the sound of loud footsteps. "Shayla? Brodie? Are you in there?"

Mike's voice! "Yes!" she called. "We're here! Your mom, Nan and Duncan, too!"

"Stay back." There was another loud bang then the door abruptly swung open, bringing a sliver of light. "Come with me," Mike urged. "Hurry!"

They moved as a group to the door. Mike and his brother Mitch stood on either side of the doorway. She wanted to throw herself into his arms, but felt self-conscious with Mike's mother and grandmother nearby.

He must not have felt the same way because he pulled her and Brodie in for a hug. "I'm so sorry," he whispered near her ear. "It's my fault you were taken."

"It wasn't, but we're safe now," she assured him, leaning against his warm strength.

"Marc and Miles brought backup," Mike said. "They've arrested four men, including Duncan's partner, Peter Fresno."

"He ratted me out," Duncan said. "I was working undercover trying to infiltrate the Dark Knights, but he wasn't buying my story—"

"We need to get out of here," Mitch said, abruptly interrupting the conversation. "Hurry!"

"Well, two of the Callahan sons are better than none," a deep voice said. "I'll get the others, too, in time."

Shayla frowned, recognizing the voice from earlier that day. The one belonging to an older man who claimed that getting the Callahans here was part of his master plan.

"Drop your guns or I'll start shooting," he continued. "I have your dear mother in my sights and from here it will be easy enough to pick the rest of you off one by one."

"Kirk Stoltz?" Mike said, his voice indicating surprise. "You? You're the one behind all of this?"

"Drop your gun, Mike," Stoltz said firmly. "You, too, Mitch. Kick them toward me. At this point, I have nothing to lose."

Mike carefully lifted his hands, showing the gun pointed toward the ceiling as he carefully bent and placed it on the floor, then kicked it with his foot over toward Stoltz. Mitch did the same thing and soon both men were unarmed.

"You were Dad's friend," Mike went on, apparently having difficulty wrapping his head around what was happening. "I don't understand how you could have been involved in his murder."

"That's because you didn't have to watch your daughter fighting for her life, only to exist in a world that can only be seen from her wheelchair." Kirk Stoltz's voice was full of anguish. "Parkerside and his equally pathetic accomplice took her from me as surely as if he'd killed her. Bad enough that my wife divorced me and remarried a guy named Alex Baker. She begged me to allow Baker to adopt Lindsey, and I eventually agreed. It worked out as Lindsey visited with me on special occasions. After the shooting, Lindsey went into a deep depression, even tried to kill herself. From that moment on, I decided the only way to get rid of the rubbish in the streets was to take care of it myself."

"Kirk, please." Margaret Callahan spoke up for the first time. "You've always been a friend to me after Max died. You shared meals at our home. Please don't do this."

"I'm sorry, Margaret, but Max had to be silenced. He was getting too close to the truth. And for a while I thought you'd all moved on. Only nosy Mike here refused to leave it alone. And then Duncan had to get into the picture." Kirk's tone hardened. "If you had just left us alone, then I wouldn't be forced to get rid of you."

Shayla instinctively moved closer to Mike's mother, as if to help calm her down. Where were the rest of the Callahans? Surely they weren't far behind.

The rat-a-tat of gunfire erupted from the apartment building above them.

"That's our cue." Stoltz's smile was evil. "Time to go."

Shayla couldn't bear to look at Mike or Mitch, worried about what might be happening above them.

If the other Callahan brothers were up there, then their chances of escaping were slim to none.

"This way, now!" Stoltz said sharply. He indicated a door not far from their locked room. Mike and Mitch exchanged panicked looks that made her wonder if the door was a surprise.

Margaret Callahan stepped forward to lead the way, but Mitch quickly came up beside her. Shayla stayed behind

Nan, still carrying Brodie, leaving Duncan and Mike to trail behind. She figured Mike and Mitch were planning some sort of move, maybe making a run for it once they were out of the basement.

But they didn't go out the way they'd come in. Instead they were led down a long, dark, winding tunnel. It was a good five minutes of walking before they reached a staircase heading up to ground level. When they were out in the sunlight, it was easy to see there was another gunman, dressed in black from head to toe, waiting for them. They were in an alley some distance from where the apartment building was located. Her hopes plummeted.

Was this it, then? Would they die here together?

"Get into the cargo van," Stoltz said. "Hurry."

The cargo van was white with Baker's Dozen written along the side in red, ending with a large glazed donut with sprinkles on the back panel.

No one would suspect this van of carrying hostages, she thought with dismay as the back door was opened by the gunman.

The moment the back door opened, several men sprang out of the van followed by a K-9. The dog clued her in on the identity of the men before she recognized Miles, Matt and Hawk.

"What the—" Stoltz's words were abruptly cut off as Mike did some sort of martial arts move that disarmed him at the same time that Matt and Hawk took care of the gunman. Duchess added her low growls to the din.

"Where's Marc?" Mike asked, not nearly as surprised to see the two Callahans and his buddy Hawk as she was.

"The feds have the apartment building under control," Miles informed them. "And look here, Noah and Maddy just arrived."

"Maddy shouldn't be here." Mike spoke up quickly. "She's pregnant."

"She is?" Margaret exclaimed, her face softening in a smile. "I'm so glad."

"Arresting me won't shut down the Dark Knights," Kirk yelled, his face flushed red with fury. "Our mission will continue!"

"No, it won't," said a deep voice from the other side of the van. Shayla glanced around in surprise when she saw her father standing there, leaning heavily on a cane.

"Daddy!" She instantly rushed to his side, shifting Brodie so that she could put her arm around his seemingly frail shoulders. "What are you doing out of the hospital?"

"I checked myself out and asked Duncan's buddy Ryker Tillman to bring me here." She noticed the tall dark-haired man standing silently beside her father, recognizing him as her brother's friend. "After Miles clued in Gordon Beecher, who in turn told me what was going on, I had to come," her father explained. "I couldn't bear the thought that my request to work undercover may have caused my son's death."

"I'll survive," Duncan said, making his way over to join them. Her eyes misted as Duncan gave their father a quick hug. She felt Mike's gaze and saw the flash of guilt in his green eyes.

He'd been wrong, just as she'd told him all along. But she wasn't angry. They'd both suffered enough over the past four years.

It was time to put the past behind them and to focus on the future. Even one that meant sharing custody of Brodie.

"You'll shut down the Dark Knights, Stoltz," her father continued, spearing Kirk with a stern look. "You're going to give us every name of the players involved, dirty cops and civilians alike."

"Why would I do that?" Stoltz said with a sneer.

"Because if you don't, I'll make sure you get placed in a prison with local criminals who will know all about you. I'm sure they'll love to meet you up close and personal."

Stoltz stared at his boss as if trying to see if he was bluffing. Shayla knew he wasn't.

"Dad, we need to get you back to the hospital."

Her father, along with everyone else, ignored her. His gaze never left Stoltz's. "If you cooperate, I can make sure you get sent to a prison where no one knows you. It's better than you deserve for all the people you've killed."

"I didn't kill Max Callahan," Stoltz protested.

"You may not have pulled the trigger," her father agreed sardonically, "but you're the one who ordered the hit."

Shayla noticed a hint of surprise in the older man's eyes.

"Yeah, that's right. We've figured it out, down to the last detail. And we'll prove it, too. We already picked up your prints at the Callahan home. Do yourself a favor and tell us what we want to hear."

Stoltz's shoulders slumped in defeat. "Fine."

"Who pulled the trigger?" Mike asked abruptly.

There was a long moment of silence as all gazes landed on Stoltz.

"I need to know," Mike insisted. "Tell me!"

Another long pause, then finally Stoltz shrugged. "Eddie Jarvis."

"And he did it on your direction, right?" Mike persisted.

The older man shrugged and looked away.

Her father sagged against her. "Daddy? Are you okay?"

Instantly, Margaret Callahan hurried over. "Ian? Didn't I hear something about you having open-heart surgery? Shayla is right. You need to go back to the hospital."

"They were going to discharge me tomorrow anyway," he groused. But Shayla noticed how her father's gaze lingered a bit on Margaret Callahan with a spark of interest.

She hid a smile as she turned toward Mike. Brodie was wiggling in her arms as if tired of being held for so long. She wanted to hand the child over to his father.

But it was too late. Mike had turned and walked away.

EIGHTEEN

Mike couldn't hear anything beyond the loud roaring in his ears. He'd been so wrong. About Ian and Duncan O'Hare. About who'd been responsible for his father's death. About his plan to investigate his father's murder all by himself like the lone wolf his family had dubbed him.

His narrow-minded, pigheaded stubbornness had almost got everyone he loved killed. And that didn't even include the three years he missed of Brodie's life.

All this time it had been Kirk Stoltz. Sure, Jarvis had pulled the trigger, but he knew that his father's friend had been the one to give the directive. Two men he'd known for years.

How had he got it so wrong?

"What's going on?" Marc asked as he walked toward him wearing a blue FBI windbreaker. Mike could see the apartment building wasn't as far away as he'd first thought. "Someone get hurt?"

Mike pulled himself together. "No, except for Shayla's brother, Duncan. He looks pretty beat-up, but he's moving okay. Probably should have one of the paramedics look at him. Otherwise, everyone's fine."

"So why the long face?" Marc asked, perplexed. "You look like you lost your best friend."

I did.

For a moment he was worried he'd spoken out loud. But Marc's quizzical gaze never wavered.

"I appreciate your help in getting the feds involved in the raid," he said, changing the subject. "Mom and Nan are fine. Good thing you found the van or he may have got away with it. There was a secret tunnel that didn't show up on Mitch's blueprints, which must be how Stoltz and the other Dark Knights were getting in and out without being seen. How long will you be tied up here?"

"A few hours yet," Marc admitted. "We'll need to take statements from everyone involved, including you."

"Yeah." Mike understood from the academy that law enforcement always included a lot of paperwork. To be fair, being a private investigator wasn't that different. He often wondered how things might have been different if he'd taken a job as a Milwaukee cop. He pulled his thoughts to the present. "Is there any way you can expedite the statements from Mom, Nan, Shayla and Brodie? They're exhausted and have already been through a lot. The little guy needs to eat soon."

"Of course." Marc's puzzled expression remained. "Come on, bro. Spill. What's bugging you?"

Mike shook his head, feeling helpless. "It's my fault. All of it."

"Funny," Marc said. "I thought for sure the Dark Knights were responsible. I've just learned that Kirk Stoltz was the leader of the pack and your old acquaintance from the academy Eddie Jarvis pulled the trigger."

Mike stared at his oldest brother, wondering how the family would feel if they knew everything he'd done. How he'd pushed Shayla away when she was pregnant and alone. How he'd selfishly helped himself to their evidence, then managed to miss key clues that could have uncovered all of this so much sooner.

How this only proved what he'd always known. That he was the worst son in the Callahan clan.

His vision blurred and he realized there were tears in his eyes. He turned and blinked them away, walking blindly, aware only of the need to get away.

"Mike? *Michael!*" The use of his full name, usually only said by his mother when he was young and had got into trouble, made him pause. He swiped at his eyes and glanced warily over his shoulder.

Shayla was struggling with Brodie while trying to catch up to him. Even knowing how much she must resent him, he couldn't ignore her. "Something wrong with Brodie?"

"Yes. He's heavy and I'm afraid to put him down with all the cops milling about." She huffed a bit as she joined him. "I need you to take him."

He hesitated, surprised by her request, and she mistook the pause for unwillingness.

"What, you thought that you'd only get to do the fun stuff?" She sounded cranky and out of sorts. Frankly, he couldn't blame her. "It's your turn. Where are you going anyway?"

"Nowhere. I just—" He shook his head. "Never mind. I'll take him." He reached for his son. Brodie wasn't thrilled with being carried anymore. He wiggled and kicked, trying to get out of his arms.

"Lemme down," Brodie demanded.

"Have you changed your mind?" Shayla asked, eyeing Mike warily.

He didn't follow her question at first, until she lifted her chin toward Brodie. He realized that while losing Shayla was like losing his arm, he still had his son.

Too bad, he wanted more. He wanted them to be a family. He loved Shayla. But didn't deserve her.

"No, I didn't change my mind." He straightened his shoulders. "I'm sorry, Shayla."

"For walking away from me just now? You should be."

"No." He winced. "I mean, yes, that, too. But more for believing the worst about your father and your brother four years ago."

She nodded thoughtfully. "You were wrong to do that, Mike," she said honestly. "But I thought we'd moved past that already. I thought…" Her voice trailed off and she looked away.

"Down!" Brodie said again. Both parents ignored him.

"It's not just that," Mike said, trying to read her body language. For a cop turned private investigator, he had trouble figuring out what was going on behind her deep brown eyes. "All this time I wasted. With you, with Brodie. I want to go back in time and kick my younger self to knock some sense into him. I made so many mistakes."

She dragged her gaze up to meet his. "We both made mistakes. But they don't matter anymore. Weren't you the one who taught me to have faith? To believe in God's plan? We're safe, Mike. You and your brothers saved us. That outweighs your past mistakes in my book."

A flicker of hope caught in his heart. "You mean that?"

"I do." A smile tugged at the corner of her mouth. "Walk back with me. I'm still worried about my dad—I can't believe he checked himself out of the hospital. I want to take him home, but apparently we can't leave yet."

"Stop right there," a voice from behind Mike said.

He froze when he felt the nose of a gun poke into his back. He wanted to turn and look, but didn't want to make any sudden movements that might cause the guy to shoot. Especially since he was still carrying Brodie.

"What do you want?" Mike asked.

"You and the kid are going to help me get out of here."

Shayla slid closer to him, so that Brodie was between

them, and he wanted to scream at her to get away. But he knew that would be useless.

She wasn't going to leave their son.

"Turn a bit to your right and start walking," the voice said. "Do anything funny and I'll shoot you here and now."

"Who are you?" Mike asked in a vain attempt to stall for time. There were dozens of cops and FBI agents swarming the place. How was it that no one noticed the guy behind him?

"Come on, Mikey. I'm hurt that you forgot all about me. Didn't our time at the academy mean anything to you?"

The use of the nickname he hated had the identity of the guy clicking into place. "Eddie Jarvis."

"Guess you're smarter than you look. Keep walking."

Mike did as he was told, although he wanted to do something, anything, to draw some attention to them. The man who'd killed his father was attempting to escape. This would be a good time for Brodie to put up a fuss, but the child had turned quiet the minute Jarvis had sneaked up behind them.

"You're a mean man!" Brodie shouted, and abruptly burst into tears.

Several things happened at once. Duchess came flying toward them, leaping at Jarvis at the same time Shayla pulled Brodie out of Mike's arms. Free of the child, he was able to spin around, using a roundhouse kick to clip Jarvis beneath the chin.

Jarvis went down to the ground, dropping his gun and screaming as the K-9 growled in his face.

Matt rushed over and picked up the weapon. "Hold him, Dutch. Hey, how in the world did he get hold of an FBI jacket?"

Marc ran toward them, his expression furious. "I just

heard over the radio that one of my men, a guy named Calderone, was knocked unconscious, and his jacket taken. Jarvis must have been the one who hit him."

"Are you sure you have all the bad guys put away?" Mike asked dryly. "For real this time?"

"Yeah. Call off your partner," Marc told Matt. "I'll take it from here."

Mike turned to Shayla and Brodie. She was doing her best to soothe the distraught child.

"He was the one who grabbed us at the cabin," she told him. "Brodie must have recognized him."

"So did Duchess," Matt agreed. "She went wild. It took me a minute to figure out you were in danger in the middle of all these cops."

"That was close." Mike shuddered, thinking about how they'd all almost died for the second time that day. This was getting old and he was done with the madness. "Listen, Marc. I'm taking Shayla, Brodie, Mom and Nan to Mom's house. You can meet us there for our statements, okay?"

Marc finished handcuffing Jarvis before glancing up at him. "Go ahead. I'll smooth it over with the brass."

"Thanks." He turned to Shayla and once again took Brodie into his arms. "We're out of here."

Shayla was exhausted, but since Margaret and Nan were still going strong, she tried to keep up. Her dad had refused to go back to the hospital, but had agreed to come with them to the Callahan matriarch's home. Duncan's friend Ryker Tillman had agreed to drive him and Duncan there.

After calling the hospital to talk to Dr. Torres and getting her father's prescriptions and follow-up appointments squared away, she returned to the kitchen to find Margaret fussing over her father.

The FBI investigators had thankfully come and gone. They'd found plenty of evidence to substantiate their story, blood from Duncan's wounds and crumbs from Brodie's fish crackers in the basement. Duncan's blood was also found outside Peter Fresno's home, corroborating her brother's side of the story. The FBI claimed that several of the cops, especially Scarletti, had begun to talk in the hope of getting a lighter sentence. Jarvis had been arrested, too, and would stand trial along with Kirk Stoltz for killing Police Chief Max Callahan.

The danger was over, but Shayla still didn't know what her and Brodie's future held.

"Oh, Shayla, I'm glad you're here. I'm heating up a batch of my famous homemade soup. Would you and Brodie like some, too? Everyone else is joining us," Margaret said.

"That would be nice, thank you. I'm sure Brodie is hungry." She'd found it difficult to look Mike's mother in the eye, worried what she and Nan would think when they discovered the truth about Brodie being Mike's son. No one held shotgun weddings anymore, did they? Nah, but she still didn't want to see disappointment or disapproval in their eyes.

Mike had pulled out toys for Brodie to play with, which had helped keep him busy. The rest of the family began to arrive—Lacy and her son, Rory; Kari and her two children, Max and Maggie; Paige and her daughter, Abby, and her son, Adam. Mitch's new wife, Dana, came with Maddy and Noah and, from the way Noah was hovering over his wife, she suspected the news about the baby was out.

Even Duncan had been welcomed. When Lacy finished patching his wounds, her brother stood next to

Ryker Tillman, the two men watching the interaction between the family members with bemusement.

"You wanna play wif me?" Brodie asked Max. Max was a year younger, but the two boys didn't seem to care.

It hit her then, that these kids were Brodie's cousins. Not all by blood, since she'd learned through conversation that a few of the children had been legally adopted, but they were Callahans just the same.

Her chest went tight and she quickly jumped up from the table and headed outside.

"Shayla?" Mike's voice came from behind. "Are you okay?"

No, she wasn't okay. But she reluctantly turned to face him. "We better tell your mother and grandmother the truth about Brodie. They deserve to know they have another grandchild."

"I don't want to talk about my mother, grandmother or Brodie," Mike said, stepping closer. "I want to talk about us."

"About how we'll manage our cocustody arrangements," she said with a nod. "I understand. Seeing Brodie with his cousins made me realize that it's best if I move back to Milwaukee."

"Shayla, I'm thrilled you're considering that, but I want you to know that I can just as easily move to Nashville." Mike's expression was serious.

She was touched by the offer, but her father and brother were here anyway, as well as the rest of Mike's family. "I'll move back. My job can be done remotely, so it's not a big deal. Besides, it's better that I keep an eye on my dad. He'll work himself to death if I don't."

"So where does that leave us?" Mike asked, reaching out to capture her hand. "I know I don't deserve you, and that I've messed up, but I was hoping you'd give me a second chance."

She eyed him warily. "Are you sure you're not just saying that because of Brodie?"

Confusion flickered in his eyes. "What do you mean?"

She waved a hand at his mother's house. "It's obvious that family plays a big role in your life. I suspect that if we didn't have Brodie, you wouldn't be standing here, asking for another chance."

"That's not true. I'm asking because, despite how badly I messed things up, I love you. I haven't been out with anyone in the four years you've been gone."

"Really?" She could hardly believe it. She'd gone out on a few dates, but none had worked out. After a year or so, she'd given up dating, period.

"Yeah, really." The truth was in his eyes. "I don't blame you for needing time, especially after the way I treated your family. But I'll do anything to make it up to you."

"As I said before, we both made mistakes."

He tugged on her hand, bringing her into his arms. "My mistakes were far worse. I've been thinking of becoming a cop, if they'll have me. Being a private investigator doesn't offer me the benefits I'll need in the future."

There he went again, mixing his duty of being Brodie's father with the potential of a relationship.

As if he read her mind, he tightened his grip on her hand. "I love you, Shayla. I love Brodie, too, but I wouldn't ask for a second chance if I didn't love *you*. If you want to know the truth, I've always loved you."

He had? The truth shimmered in his eyes, so she wrapped her hands around his neck and smiled, believing him. "I don't need time, Mike. Because I love you, too."

"Are you sure?" His gaze was full of hope and wonder.

"Kiss me," she said, tugging his head down to hers.

He readily obliged. When they finally came up for air, he cradled her close. "We're going to do it right this time," he whispered in her ear.

"We are?" She leaned back, looking into his eyes.

"Yes." He smiled broadly. "Shayla Louise O'Hare, will you please marry me?"

"I'd be honored to marry you, Michael Jerome Callahan," she said with a smile.

"I'm glad." Mike kissed her again, sweetly. "No secret courthouse plans this time. I want to marry you in our family's church, with both of our families in attendance."

The picture that came to her mind made her sigh. "I'd like that. But we have to wait until my dad is healthy enough to walk me down the aisle."

"Agreed. But not too long, Brodie needs a younger brother or sister."

The idea of more children with Mike made her smile. "I want Brodie to grow up believing in God. And maybe we can work on my dad and Duncan along the way."

"I'm up for the challenge," Mike agreed.

"By the way, did you see how your mom seems to be doting on my dad?" Shayla asked.

Mike winced. "I did," he acknowledged. "But I'd rather not think about them dating, if you don't mind."

She giggled. "Hey, as long as they're happy, who are we to interfere?"

"I guess you're right." He shrugged, then gestured toward the house. "Come on, let's tell the family about Brodie."

She held back. "Now? With everyone here?"

"Shayla, my mother and grandmother are going to be thrilled to know I'm finally settling down. That I'm no longer a lone wolf. That Brodie is our son. Please trust me on this."

She drew in a deep breath and let it out slowly. "Okay. Let's do it."

Mike kept her hand in his as they entered the house. "Mom? Nan? Mr. O'Hare? Will you join us in the living room for a minute?"

Shayla wondered if Mike noticed the way his mother helped her father into the great room, staying close to his side.

"I—we have an announcement to make," Mike said with a broad smile. "Shayla has agreed to marry me. And if you were wondering…yes, Brodie is our son." There was a moment of silence so he added, "Our biological son."

"I'm aware of that, dear," Margaret said, patting his arm. "Impossible to miss since Brodie looks just like you did at that age. Solid and sturdy. For years you constantly complained about being hungry."

"I'm hungry," Brodie announced, gazing around at the adults. "Time to eat?"

That made the entire room crack up with laughter.

"Yippee skippy," Maddy said with a smile. "The lone-wolf Callahan has bitten the dust." She rested her hand protectively on her still-flat abdomen, Noah cuddling her close.

Dana leaned on Mitch, too, and the way he placed his hand over her lower abdomen and the secret smile they shared made her suspect another baby announcement would be forthcoming. Mike was right—they needed to jump on the grandbaby train before it left without them.

Shayla caught her father's gaze. He gave her a smile and a nod in approval.

Amid the chorus of congratulations and well-wishing, she knew in her heart that this was what she'd hoped for since the moment she'd reunited with Mike. Her dream had come true.

She and Brodie would become Callahans for real.

A sense of peace washed over her. In that moment she knew that God was up in Heaven beaming down at them with love.

Pleased that another member of His flock had come home.

* * * * *

If you enjoyed this story, look for the other books in the Callahan Confidential series:

Shielding His Christmas Witness
The Only Witness
Christmas Amnesia
Shattered Lullaby
Primary Suspect

And pick up these other exciting stories from Laura Scott:

Wrongly Accused
Down to the Wire
Under the Lawman's Protection
Forgotten Memories
Holiday on the Run
Mirror Image

Available now from Love Inspired Suspense!

Find more great reads at www.LoveInspired.com.

Dear Reader,

Protecting His Secret Son is the sixth and last book in my Callahan Confidential series. I know you have been waiting for Mike's story and, as you expected, I was thrilled to finally solve Max Callahan's murder.

I hope you enjoyed Mike and Shayla's story. Many of you have reached out asking about Hawk's story, so I'm hoping to write his book very soon. I love hearing from my readers. If you're interested in contacting me or signing up for my newsletter, please visit my website at www.laurascottbooks.com. I'm also on Facebook at Laura Scott Books Author and on Twitter @laurascottbooks.

Yours in faith,
Laura Scott

COMING NEXT MONTH FROM
Love Inspired® Suspense

Available March 5, 2019

AMISH HAVEN
Amish Witness Protection • by Dana R. Lynn
When criminal lawyer Tyler Everson witnesses a murder, he becomes the killer's next target—along with his estranged wife, Annabelle, and their daughter. Now they must enter witness protection in Amish country. But will going into hiding keep them safe...and bring the family back together?

DANGEROUS SANCTUARY
FBI: Special Crimes Unit • by Shirlee McCoy
FBI agent Radley Tumberg must rescue his fellow agent, Honor Remington, from a spiritual sanctuary where she's being held against her will. But when he reaches her, can they work together to escape the sanctuary and find evidence that its leader isn't what he's pretending to be?

BURIED MOUNTAIN SECRETS
by Terri Reed
While searching for her missing brother in the mountains near their home, Maya Gallo finds herself caught between treasure hunters and the bounty they'll kill for. But with help from mounted patrol deputy Alex Trevino, she might be able to save her brother...and stay alive.

MURDER MIX-UP
by Lisa Phillips
After a man is killed while carrying a navy ID belonging to Secret Service agent Declan Stringer's brother, Declan is determined to figure out why. Even if it means turning a killer's sights on him...and convincing NCIS agent Portia Finch he'd make a great temporary partner.

INNOCENT TARGET
by Elisabeth Rees
Journalist Kitty Linklater knows her father isn't a murderer, and she plans to prove it—especially after the town turns on her and someone becomes determined to silence her. Chief Deputy Ryan Lawrence doesn't believe in her father's innocence, but he'll risk his life to guard her.

SHATTERED TRUST
by Sara K. Parker
After Natalie Harper was left at the altar, enjoying her honeymoon alone is the best way to cope—until she's attacked on the beach. Luke Everett, the bodyguard hired by her federal judge father, arrives just in time to ensure she survives. But can he figure out why the assailant's after her?

LOOK FOR THESE AND OTHER LOVE INSPIRED BOOKS WHEREVER BOOKS ARE SOLD, INCLUDING MOST BOOKSTORES, SUPERMARKETS, DISCOUNT STORES AND DRUGSTORES.

LISCNM0219

SPECIAL EXCERPT FROM

Love Inspired
SUSPENSE

*When her son witnesses a murder, Julia Bradford and
her children must go into witness protection with the
Amish. Can former police officer Abraham King keep
them safe at his Amish farm?*

Read on for a sneak preview of
Amish Safe House *by Debby Giusti,*
the exciting continuation of the
Amish Witness Protection miniseries,
available February 2019 from Love Inspired Suspense!

"I have your new identities." US marshal Jonathan Mast
sat across the table from Julia in the hotel where she and
her children had been holed up for the last five days.

The Luchadors wanted to kill William so he wouldn't
testify against their leader. As much as Julia didn't trust
law enforcement, she had to rely on the US Marshals and
their witness protection program to keep her family safe.
No wonder her nerves were stretched thin.

"We're ready to transport you and the children,"
Jonathan Mast continued. "We'll fly into Kansas City
tonight, then drive to Topeka and north to Yoder."

"What's in Kansas?"

Jonathan pulled out his phone and accessed a
photograph. He handed the cell to Julia. "Abraham King
will watch over you in Kansas."

Julia studied the picture. The man looked to be in his midthirties with a square face and deep-set eyes beneath dark brows. His nose appeared a bit off center, as if it had been broken. Lips pulled tight and no hint of a smile on his angular face.

"Mr. King doesn't look happy."

Jonathan shrugged. "Law enforcement photos are never flattering."

Her stomach tightened. "He's a cop?"

"Past tense. He left the force three years ago."

Once a cop, always a cop. Her ex had been a police officer. He'd protected others but failed to show that same sense of concern when it came to his own family. The marshal seemed oblivious to her unease.

"Abe is an old friend," Jonathan continued. "A widower from my police-force days who owns a farm and has a spare house on his property. He lives in a rural Amish community."

"Amish?"

"That's right."

"Bonnets and buggies?" she asked.

He smiled weakly. "You'll be off the grid, Mrs. Bradford. No one will look for you there."

Don't miss
Amish Safe House *by Debby Giusti,*
available February 2019 wherever
Love Inspired® Suspense books and ebooks are sold.

www.LoveInspired.com

Copyright © 2019 by Harlequin Books S.A.

LISEXP0119